EMERGENCY!

Hank Dekker was half-asleep when the realization hit him like a two-fisted punch in the gut: "I'm sinking!"

It was true. Just nine days into his 2,400-mile passage across the Pacific Ocean, Hank had sailed smack into Hurricane Henrietta. As Hank woke up and sized up the situation, he remembered that he had left one of *Dark Star*'s two sails up when he went to sleep.

"The jib [small sail] was under water," Hank recalled. "I realized that if I didn't get outside the boat and release it, *Dark Star* would sink." To do that, Hank would have to make his way out of the cabin. He would be exposed to the wind and waves as he untied the sail. This would be a very hard thing for any person to do. Because of his blindness, it would be even tougher for Hank.

*

Be awed by the determination and real-life adventures of: Todd Skinner, a rock climber stranded without food during an Amazon ascent; Team American Pride, which took on the world's most grueling endurance event — the Raid Gauloises; Beth Rypins, who challenged frigid waters on a Siberian kayaking trip; and sailor Hank Dekker, who crossed the Pacific solo.

Forget about playing to win. All of these athletes play to *survive*!

For Calene, who is wonderful.
And for Devin and Connor,
who are adventurous.

ON THE Edge

Four true stories of extreme outdoor sports adventures

By Martin Dugard

A *Sports Illustrated For Kids* Book

BANTAM BOOKS

TORONTO • NEW YORK • LONDON • SYDNEY • AUCKLAND

On the Edge by Martin Dugard

A Bantam Book/June 1995

Cover and interior design by Miriam Dustin
Front cover photograph of Todd Skinner by Galen Rowell/Mountain Light
Back cover photographof Beth Rypins by John D. Berry
Maps illustrated by Carol M. Vidinghoff

For information address: Bantam Books

ISBN 0-553-48310-2

Published simultaneously in the United States and Canada

Bantam books are published by Bantam Books, a division of Bantam Doubleday Dell Publishing Group, Inc. Its trademark, consisting of the words "Bantam Books" and the portrayal of a rooster, is Registered in the U.S. Patent and Trademark Office and in other countries. Marca Registrada. Bantam Books, 1540 Broadway, New York, NY 10036

Printed in the United States of America

CWO 10 9 8 7 6 5 4 3 2 1

CONTENTS *

HARD ROCK

A CLIMBING EXPEDITION'S STRUGGLE TO SURVIVE AN AMAZON ASCENT

1 * A LONG WAY FROM WYOMING

Rock climber Todd Skinner sighed as he checked his ropes and pulled a pair of binoculars from his backpack. He was 500 feet above the ground, dangling on the craggy granite face of Mount Aritityope *{air-ee-ti-tee-opay}*, which is in South America between the countries of Brazil and Venezuela. He felt more hungry than he ever had in his life. Todd was very tired, too. Anxiously, he raised the binoculars to his eyes and scanned the earth below.

"See anything?" his climbing partner, Paul Piana,

Todd Skinner (right) and Paul Piana conquered the challenge of the slick face of California's El Capitan before taking on Mount Aritityope.

BILL HATCHER

called out. Paul was 10 feet below Todd, carefully making his way upward as he talked.

"Nothing but jungle, buddy," Todd replied with frustration. "Nothing but jungle."

And it was true. As far as Todd looked in every direction, all he could see was the emerald green carpet of the Amazon River Basin, which is the largest jungle in the world. Green, green, green, everywhere he looked. Which was why Todd was so frustrated. The color Todd was looking for was dark blue — dark blue parachutes.

When Todd and Paul and their team started their expedition to climb Mt. Aritityope almost three weeks earlier, they had dropped their food in by parachute. But now they couldn't find the parachutes and the 23-person expedition was starving to death as a result. Todd and Paul had each lost 15 pounds from their 150-pound frames. One member of their group, French climber Monique *{mo-NEEK}* Delmasso, had grown so weak from lack of food that she couldn't even walk!

So while the rest of the expedition searched on the ground for the parachutes, Todd and Paul looked from above. After five days of fruitless looking, though, their situation was beginning to seem hopeless. Todd quietly wondered if they would all die in the jungle, never to be found again.

"That it?" Todd mumbled, pointing to a light patch of jungle. Normally quick with a joke, he could barely talk from lack of nourishment. His thickly muscled forearms and shoulders had become skinny and not as quick to power his body up the mountain.

Paul peered at the spot. He had finally climbed up next to Todd on the face. "Nope. Looks like a low cloud or something," he said. Paul grinned weakly and tried to sound playful. "Even so, isn't this a swell weight-loss program?"

Todd laughed, despite his misery. Looking at Paul, Todd remembered that they had been in other tight spots together, and had gotten out of them. Todd knew that the best way to deal with tough situations was to keep a good attitude. "The beauty of this trip," Todd replied in the best joking manner he could manage, "is that things are going wrong. A trip doesn't become an adventure until something goes wrong."

Thinking back, Todd realized that only three months before, the two Wyoming natives had never even heard of Mount Aritityope. For that matter, very few other people had, either. Shaped just like a 2,500-foot high shark's fin, Aritityope is located deep in the Amazon River Basin. It's more than 1,000 miles from the nearest city and the mountain is so remote that geologists (people who study rocks and rock formations) have never examined it.

Todd and Paul first heard about Aritityope when an expedition organizer named Rick Ridgeway approached them about climbing to the top of it. The kind of expeditions or trips Rick organizes involve large groups of people traveling to remote areas of the world in search of great adventure. Rick had seen this particular mountain from an airplane several years before. Looking at the big

VENEZUELA
GUYANA
SURINAME
COLOMBIA
FRENCH
GUIANA
ECUADOR
MT. ARITITYOPE
BRAZIL
PERU
BOLIVIA
E-Q-U-A-
PARAGUAY
T-O-R-
CHILE
URUGUAY
ARGENTINA
SOUTH AMERICA

gray fin rising dramatically up out of the jungle, he promised himself he would come back some day. Though Rick's job took him to other places around the world in the next few years, he couldn't get Aritityope out of his mind. It was so grand and stunning. The best part was, it had never been climbed before. Finally, he decided the best thing to do was make a movie about people climbing it. The two people Rick had in mind? Todd and Paul. They were among the best rock climbers in the world. It would be the chance of a lifetime.

"No," Todd replied when Rick asked them if they wanted to make the climb. "I'm too busy." Paul said the same thing. But Rick wasn't put off that easily. When Todd left for Asia on a two-month-long climbing trip, Rick called Paul almost every day to ask if they would please come and climb Aritityope. Finally, Paul gave in. When Todd came back from Asia, Paul told him the news.

"I signed us up to climb in South America," Paul said.

Todd raised an eyebrow. "Really?" he asked.

"Really. Oh, by the way, we leave in ten days."

"Why not?" Todd laughed, knowing that Paul shared his great taste for adventure. "Expeditions are like planets," Todd thought later, trying to figure out why he'd agreed so easily after saying "no" before. "They have a gravity all their own that causes you to get excited about going and what you're gonna do once you get there. Sooner or later, that gravity just sucks you in. The next thing you know, you're on the plane."

On the flight to South America, Todd thought about the dangers. Rick's plan was to travel up the Amazon and Orinoco Rivers by canoe, then hike through the rain forest (which is another name for jungle) to the bottom of Aritityope. And though the river is home to flesh-eating fish called piranhas and to alligators, its hazards aren't much compared with those in the rain forest.

Walking where no man had been before, the team would have to clear a path with long knives called machetes *{ma-SHET-eez}*. It would come upon everything from poisonous snakes to stinging scorpions to fierce jaguars. "You couldn't touch anything in the rain forest," Todd marveled later. "Even regular-looking vines had a poison on them that ate away at your skin."

Once their plane landed in Caracas, Venezuela, Todd and Paul met the rest of the expedition. Even though Todd and Paul would be doing the climbing, a lot of other people were necessary to make their trip happen. There were local Indians called the Jicuanas *{Hick-wan-uz}*, who would carry supplies. Rick was there, too, along with his cameraman. Two other climbers came along to help out. One was the French climber, Monique Delmasso. The other was named Kiké *{Kee-kay}* Arnal. He was from Venezuela and was chosen because he climbed often in the rain forest.

Even though the whole group numbered 21 people, Rick decided at the last minute to add two more Indians from another tribe. They were known as Yanamanis *{ya-*

nuh-MAH-neez) and they would help as jungle guides. Later on, Rick was very glad that he made that decision.

With the group completely assembled, it was time to make final preparations. "Hey, Todd," Rick called out as he looked at the group. "Could you be in charge of buying all the food?"

"Sure," Todd replied. With that, he and Paul left for the local marketplace to purchase four weeks worth of supplies.

But when they brought it all back, Todd immediately saw that there was a big problem. The combination of food, climbing gear, and camera and radio equipment weighed almost a ton. "This is a mountain of stuff," Todd pointed out to Rick, "and those Indians don't weigh more than a hundred pounds apiece, so they can't carry very much. I mean, it would take about 50 of them to carry all this." Todd tried to come up with a solution. It was almost noon and the equatorial sun burned on his face. The thought of lugging those supplies through this same heat seemed like an impossible task.

"So what are you saying?" Rick asked. As organizer, he was responsible for everything from making sure the expedition had enough food to making sure it had enough flashlight batteries. He was the one who paid the Indians for the work and rented the boats that would take them up river. The success or failure of the trip rested on his shoulders. If even the slightest thing went wrong, he would get the blame.

Todd took a deep breath before saying what he had on

his mind. He knew Rick wouldn't like the idea very much, but it was the only way. "If we're gonna get this stuff into the mountain, we're gonna have to drop it in by parachute."

"Parachute?" Rick said in disbelief. Todd had been right — Rick didn't like the idea one bit.

"Parachute."

"What if we don't find them?" Rick replied. "The rain forest is really thick. If we don't find that food, we'll starve."

"Relax, we'll find the chutes," Todd answered, crossing his fingers for luck.

But three weeks later as he hung on the face of Aritityope and scanned the jungle below with his binoculars, Todd winced at the memory of those words. All he knew was that he and the other climbers had been in the plane together and had watched the parachutes drop down, and now he couldn't find them.

"What should we do?" Paul asked.

"Only thing we can do," Todd replied grimly. "Climb higher and hope we see them from above." Slowly, with great effort, Todd pushed off on a toehold and began climbing again.

2 * Growing Up Cowboy

Todd had a secret weapon in his battle to save the expedition: his upbringing. He was raised on a ranch in Pinedale, Wyoming. Every day was a new learning experience about the rigors of living outdoors. "Growing up as a cowboy prepared me for stuff like this," he said in reference to jungle life. "It taught me to persevere."

Like Huckleberry Finn, Todd was more comfortable outdoors than inside. Every day, he rode horses, went fishing and hunting, and sometimes even climbed to the top of the mountains around his house. "I lived at the base of the Wind River Range," he remembers fondly. "My life revolved around the local mountains." When Todd would go mountain climbing, it was usually with his Dad, who ran a wilderness school for people who wanted to learn about outdoor life. In those days, it was common for climbers to use hammers to force heavy metal spikes called pitons *(pee-tons)* into the face of the mountain. As they climbed, they attached special rope ladders to the spikes. To climb the mountain, all they had to do was climb the ladder.

When he was 14, Todd began to get tired of climbing mountains. Climbing a rope ladder wasn't as thrilling to him as it once was. "I noticed that I had a lot more fun just climbing local boulders," Todd says. "I didn't use any equipment, all I had to do was climb. It was a lot more scary and difficult to climb without all that gear, but I had a great time. After awhile, that was all I wanted to do."

Todd didn't know it, but he had stumbled onto a new sport. It was called free-climbing (see box on page 17). In this sport, climbers travel up the face of a rock without rope ladders. Instead, they wedge their hands and feet into the little cracks and ledges that cover rock faces. Often that meant holding on by nothing other than their fingertips!

By the time Todd left the ranch four years later to attend the University of Wyoming, he had developed the strong shoulders and forearms that are the trademark of a good free-climber. Still, he didn't know free-climbing was a sport until he visited a local wall known as Vedauwoo *{VEED-a-voo}* and met other climbers who were practicing there. Todd was so excited! He began spending every spare minute he could at Vedauwoo, trying to become the best rock climber he could.

"Climbing became part of my college experience," Todd says now. "Just as important as spending time in the classroom. It's where I learned how far it was possible to push myself." Even when he wasn't climbing, Todd worked to make himself a better climber. He began stretching every day to make himself more flexible. To get stronger, he did fingertip pull-ups.

Free-climbing is not entirely free of equipment. The climbers still need to be attached to a rope for safety. The difference is that free-climbers don't use the rope to pull themselves up the way aided mountain climbers do. Free-climbers climb up, and then insert either metal wedges or special anchors called "cams" into cracks in the rock. They clip the ropes onto the cams and wedges, and then continue up. If they fall, the ropes catch them.

Walking into the school cafeteria one day, Todd was surprised to see a climber making his way up the outside of the building. Todd watched him for a minute. He could tell the climber was very good. "What's your name?" Todd finally called out.

"Paul Piana," came the reply.

Thin and muscular like Todd, dark-haired Paul was also every bit as crazy about climbing. Also like Todd, Paul grew up on a ranch in Wyoming and began climbing at about the age of 8. The two hit it off right away. Soon they climbed together all the time. Most of the rocks were small. When they climbed bigger rocks — some that were a hundred feet high — they learned how to use safety ropes and anchor them to the cams and wedges. The more they climbed, the better they got. And as they got better, Todd began having some wild dreams. "I began to think we could climb big walls — really big walls. Walls no one had ever climbed before."

Like dreamers everywhere, Todd kept those thoughts to himself for fear they would sound crazy. But soon Paul mentioned that he was thinking the same thing. "Because nobody had ever done it before, we had nobody to tell us we couldn't do it," Todd points out, "so we went ahead and started planning." They began looking for a very special wall, one that would push them to their mental, physical, and emotional limits.

What they found was El Capitan. Set in California's majestic Yosemite Valley, El Cap is over 3,000 feet of slick vertical rock. To make the climb even tougher, the two last sections before the top are the most difficult. Some said El Cap could never be conquered.

Unable to think of anything else, Todd and Paul trained for two years during and after college. Their muscles became more powerful and their reflexes became quicker. They practiced every day. When they decided it was time to take a shot at El Capitan, they were sure they would succeed. "I knew we were ready to do it because we were as strong as we could be," Todd says proudly.

When they got to Yosemite, a popular destination for climbers, people laughed at them. "The locals wanted us to fail," says Todd, "because they had never dared to dream that wildly." Todd and Paul ignored them and began making their way up the wall. Day after day they inched toward the top of the face.

"At first it was hard getting used to being so high off the ground," Todd says, remembering what it was like to be dangling 1,000 feet above the earth. "When you're up that high, your [safety] rope seems unbelievably skinny, like there's no way it could hold you." But it did. Some days they fell two or three times. In every instance, the rope jerked taut and stopped their fall.

At night, they slept in special cots they anchored to the wall. Slowly, the two fearless cowboys unlocked the puzzle of cracks and ledges forming the perfect route to the top. Some days they would only climb 5 or 10 feet before reaching a dead end. Others they found the right combination and went as many as 500 feet.

As they climbed, Todd and Paul began to see a new

strength coming from inside themselves. They weren't as scared of falling as they used to be. Their climbing technique became smooth, refined, and focused. When times got tough, like the days when it rained or they couldn't find a good route, both of them showed an ability to laugh or tell a bad joke to relieve the tension.

Finally the day came when they could see the top just a few hundred feet above them. Instead of being happy, though, Todd and Paul were nervous. Between them and the top of El Capitan was a challenging stretch of climbing known as "The Great Barrier Roof." Instead of being upright, the face was horizonal there. To get past it, they would have to climb upside down for 25 feet, as though they were climbing across a ceiling. And that wasn't all. After they got past The Roof, Todd and Paul faced The Headwall, which tipped out from the rock the last 500 feet to the top.

A headwall is a large rock formation on a mountain face. It is steep and has few ledges for the climber to grab onto.

Paul inched onto The Roof first. He knew that a rope would catch him if he fell, but it was still scary to look down and see the ground 3,000 feet below. He felt like Spiderman. "It was an amazing struggle to control fear," Paul remembers. "Technically, it was wild, it was crazy. My feet were swinging out and I was just holding on with my hands. It was totally dynamite." Paul channeled his fear into strength. "I used the extra energy I got from all that adrenaline that the fear brought on. It helped me get a better grip on the rock."

Slowly, cautiously, Todd followed. Paul helped him by telling him the best route. Soon they were past The Roof and on to The Headwall. They wanted to relax but they knew they couldn't — The Headwall was too hard. They crept upward.

Adrenaline *[uh-DREN-uh-lynn]* is a chemical released by the body in tense situations to make the body perform better.

Other climbers watching with binoculars from the ground were amazed at what they saw: Todd and Paul were almost to the top of El Capitan! Then, with one final push, they did it. Forty-eight days after starting, Todd Skinner and Paul Piana stood atop El Capitan. They had done what everybody had said was impossible.

3 * LEAVING NORMAL

When Rick Ridgeway first mapped the trip inland to Mount Aritityope, he planned for a week of travel both ways. The trip up the Amazon and Orinoco Rivers would take four days by dugout canoe. Walking from the river through the jungle to Aritityope would take three more. But, as an experienced leader who had once taken a team to Mount Everest (which is the tallest mountain in the world), Rick always allowed room for error. His favorite method of forecasting trouble was a game called "What if?"

It was simple. Any time Rick sensed a situation

might get out of control, he asked the question, "What if?" What if we all get sick, do we have enough medicine? What if the radio's battery goes dead, do we have a spare? What if we get lost, do we have Indian guides to show us the way? Again and again, Rick played the "What if?" game as he prepared his small army to go into the jungle.

But there was one situation he forgot. What if the river is so low we can't travel by boat? "The Amazon River was fine," Todd recalls. "The water was up and it even rained on the first day." But when the expedition came to the Orinoco, the river that led directly to the mountain, its luck changed. The water level was so low that it was filled with sandbars. The adventurers often had to get out and push the boats. Instead of the four days planned, their time on the river stretched to five, then six, then seven days. Todd, the man in charge of food, began to worry. "I realized we would have to begin hunting and fishing if we were going to make it," he says.

The Yanamani Indians immediately showed how valuable they were. They pulled piranha, alligator, and 80-pound catfish from the Orinoco. For breakfast, they dug up turtle eggs that were buried in the sand. They shot wild birds with bows and arrows. "Catching alligators was the easiest part," Todd says, not sounding the slightest bit scared. "There were always four or five around the boat. At night, we would shine a flashlight on the water and see as many as ten or twelve. It began to get almost casual to have a six-foot alligator for dinner."

After eight days, the team decided to beach the canoes and start walking. To get a compass bearing toward Mount Arititiyope, Todd and one of the Yanamanis climbed to the top of a tall tree. Todd was surprised and overjoyed to see the giant shark's fin sticking up in the distance, not too far away. "Hey," he yelled down, "I can see it. It's only about fifteen miles away! We can make it in two days."

But the Yanamani was grim. He couldn't speak English, and he had a hard time understanding why Todd looked so happy. Back on the ground, he found an interpreter. The interpreter and the Yanamani pulled Todd aside. "The mountain is very, very far away. It will take us many days to get there," the interpreter relayed.

"What? How can he tell?" Todd asked with amazement.

"Because it is still blue," the interpreter said, referring to the ring of haze surrounding the mountain. "When we get close, it will not look blue anymore."

Quietly, Todd was skeptical. He had spent his whole life in the outdoors. Arititiyope looked two days away, no more.

In high spirits, the group began its march. There was no path, so machete-carrying guides hacked a trail through the thick rain forest. "The rain forest is amazing," Todd marvels. "Everything that lives there has learned to protect itself in order to survive. The plants are always sharp or poisonous. There are poisonous snakes, centipedes, scorpions, and biting ants. And even spiders so big that they eat birds. Believe me, when we were walking through there, the scariest thing I could ever imagine doing was stepping off the machete path. The plants are so thick that even five feet off the path you might not be able to find your way back. And if that happens," he pauses, remembering the fear, "if that happens, you might never be found again."

After two days, they were still nowhere near Aritityope. The Yanamani had been right. Worse, finding food was much more difficult than on the river. Although the Indians were able to shoot an occasional bird or monkey, it wasn't enough to feed the entire expedition. The hunger pangs of missed meals got worse as starvation set in. Monique was feeling it the most. Thin to begin with, her body had no extra fat to give her fuel. She entered into a catabolic state. Everyone was alarmed. They decided that to help her, they would have to push harder to get to Aritityope.

A catabolic state is one in which the muscles start to break down to provide fuel for the body.

"The parachutes were at the mountain and there was food at the parachutes," Todd points out in defense of the plan. "Even though pushing harder meant less time for the Indians to stop and hunt, we knew that the sooner we made it to the 'chutes, the quicker we could get food."

Eating nothing but wild honey for the last two days, the group finally arrived at the base of Aritityope. They were 16 days into a journey that was supposed to last 30, and they weren't even halfway through! Immediately, a hammock was prepared for Monique to rest in and a huge search party was sent to find the parachutes.

But the blue parachutes were nowhere to be found. For two days and nights, the expedition searched the treetops and jungle floor. The "What if?" question Rick had asked Todd — What if we don't find the parachutes? — was actually happening.

Then the expedition's problems went from bad to worse. A routine check of the radio revealed that it was broken. All it did was make static noises. Any hope of calling in a rescue helicopter was dashed. Either food was found immediately or the expedition would starve to death in the Amazon Rain Forest.

Todd and Paul decided to take the situation into their own hands. "What do you think?" Paul asked.

Todd was ready with his answer. "This jungle's so thick that we'll never find them on the ground. Maybe if we climb up the mountain a little bit, we can look down and see the parachutes. It was my idea to parachute all that food in. I feel like it's my responsibility to make sure we find it."

Paul looked at Todd. He trusted his judgment, but he wasn't sure that he had enough strength to climb Aritityope. Lack of food had made him tired and weak. But when he thought about Todd's logic, Paul knew he was right. The jungle *was* thick. A person might be just 10 feet from a parachute but still not be able to see it because a sea of vines and plants covered it.

"You're right," Paul finally said to Todd. "I think climbing is the only answer."

Armed with binoculars, the cowboys set out to save the expedition.

4 * Scaling the Shark

The coarse granite face of Aritityope was like no other wall Todd or Paul had climbed anywhere in the world. It was slick and covered with plants. Bushy, thorny flowers called bromeliads *{bro-mee-lee-ads}* grew straight out from the wall. They had fish-hook spines that cut into the hand of whomever tried to grab onto one. Another, more deadly hazard was "three-steppers," super-poisonous snakes that make their homes in the narrow mountain ledges. The name comes from the belief that the person they bite will be dead before he or she can take even three steps.

Before beginning the climb, Todd and Paul studied the mountain. They knew that they needed to climb it as quickly as possible. The sooner they got high enough to spot the parachutes, the better off the expedition would be. "We should start over there," Todd said, pointing to the right side of the mountain. That was where the fin started its curve. "If we start there, we can make time by climbing up the curve of the fin."

"You're right," Paul agreed. "Let's do it."

For awhile, they found easy climbing on the gentle

incline. Todd led the way, with Paul following behind to belay *{buh-LAY}*, which means to anchor the rope. The rock was slick from low clouds and light rain. Wind swirled across the face, forcing Todd to work harder to keep his balance. Sometimes he would slip because of the wind and fog, then cut his hands as he grabbed on to a bromeliad to halt his fall. He was soon scraped, cut, and bleeding. But even though the climbing was tough, Todd and Paul were tougher. Soon they were high enough to see over the tops of the trees. Anxiously, Todd pulled out the binoculars.

"See anything?" Paul asked as Todd scanned the area.

"Nothing," Todd replied, jamming the binoculars back into his pack. "Let's climb some more."

Up and up they went. Following them up the ropes were Rick and a cameraman to film the action and help them look for the parachutes. But no one ever saw anything below except the green of the jungle. Each night when the climbers anchored their cots, they could feel themselves getting more hungry and more desperate.

After two days, the curve of the fin became impassable. Todd led the way as they traversed back to the middle of the face. Traversing means that instead of going straight up the mountain, they were moving from one side across toward the other. Todd felt at home dangling from the vertical wall. It reminded him of El Capitan. He felt confident and happy.

But gloom again settled over them as the parachutes stayed hidden from sight. "Why did I ever leave

Wyoming?" he shouted in frustration when a misstep caused him to slip and almost fall. Todd didn't know it, but the sudden mood changes he was experiencing are common with people who are suffering from starvation.

Back on the ground, Monique's suffering had become so intense that she no longer had the strength to rise from her hammock. Kiké stepped up the search for the parachutes, though it looked more and more hopeless every day. "I knew exactly where they were when we dropped them in," Kiké moaned, flopping into his hammock at the end of another trying day. "Now it is like trying to find a needle in a haystack."

Meanwhile, the Indians were starting to get skeptical. They didn't believe that food had fallen from the sky, so they refused to search anymore. It was a waste of time, they said. They argued that instead of searching for parachutes, they should be out hunting. Kiké tried to convince them that it was smarter to look for the parachutes than hunt. The Indians thought he was crazy.

> A tapir looks like a giant pig but is related to the rhinoceros and horse. It makes a lot of noise when it walks.

One day, one of the Indians spotted a 600-pound tapir moving slowly through the rain forest. The Indian tried to sneak up on the animal. He knew it would be enough food for everybody, and then they wouldn't have to look for the parachutes anymore. The Indian had a bow and arrow with him, and he carried the expedition's shotgun. He only had one shotgun shell, so he couldn't afford to miss.

He fired. Shotgun pellets hit the tapir in the side. Instead of falling, however, the frightened animal charged off into the jungle. All the Indians chased after it. It wasn't until two days later that they returned to camp, looking very disappointed. They hadn't been able to find the huge beast. The expedition needed Todd and Paul to find the parachutes more than ever before.

But things were getting tough up on the mountain. Low clouds hid the ground and threatened to make the granite too slick to climb. In the distance, Todd could see a huge storm making its way toward Aritityope. The rain and wind it would bring could blow the four climbers off the face of the mountain. In effect, they were becoming stranded "between heaven and hell, and a long way from either one," as Todd put it.

The storm hit with brutal force. The four climbers were unable to continue up because the rock was too wet. The fact that they had lost strength from starvation only made the situation more miserable. Bravely, they dangled on the face and waited for the storm to pass.

Meanwhile, back on the ground, something had happened to the radio. The reason it didn't work in the first place was somewhat unusual. Built before 1975, it could only be tuned by snipping off sections of the antenna with wire clippers. The reasoning went that different lengths of antenna corresponded with different radio signals. No one in the expedition was aware of this. The only thing anyone knew was that the radio was broken and they could not call for help.

But a miraculous thing happened during the storm: A strong gust of wind swooped down on the camp. Like an invisible hand, it snapped a branch off a tree. The branch fell on the antenna, snapping off a section. In fact, it snapped the antenna so perfectly that Kiké was able to raise a missionary outpost in Brazil. He couldn't believe it! Frantically, he told the missionaries to contact authorities in Caracas, Venezuela. Rescue was on the way!

When Kiké contacted the climbing party via walkie-talkie to tell them the good news about the radio, Todd's outlook went from hopeless to happy. The other climbers' moods changed drastically, too. They could hardly believe their good luck.

"Before then," Todd says, recalling earlier walkie-talkie communications, "it was one band of starving people talking to another. There was no emotion. Long silences. We were always worried about the French woman. But when we found out about the radio, we were thrilled. Really thrilled."

After a short celebration, they realized that finding the parachutes was no longer the most important thing. What *was* important was making it to the top of Aritityope as quickly as they could. Unless they were standing right on top of the mountain, the rescue helicopter wouldn't be able to pick them up. It was crucial that they got off the face. Weak and wet, they anxiously waited out the storm and rested for the final assault on the summit.

5 * Rescue

In a replay of the El Capitan ascent, Todd and Paul's climb got toughest just before the summit. In this case, their path was blocked by a huge rock that was slick with rain and algae. Looking up, Todd thought he saw a way to the summit. It was a giant crack in the rock that looked like a chimney. "It looks awful," Todd said to Paul, "but it's not as bad as the face."

Taking another look at the clouds, then at the chimney, they pushed on. Squeezing themselves inside the giant crack, Todd and Paul maneuvered upward. It was slimy inside from algae and rain, but not so bad that they couldn't climb.

A short time later, they got their reward: After wriggling through the chimney, they were standing proudly atop Aritityope. To their left lay Brazil. To the right, Venezuela. With great ceremony, they removed a pair of cowboy hats from their packs and put them on. If the world were ever to ask, they wanted it known that Wyoming cowboys were the first men atop Mount Aritityope. Just as the rain started pouring down, they took the hats off and threw them from the summit into the rain forest far below.

A chimney is a narrow but open chute of rock. The climber wedges his or her body in it in order to climb upward.

The rescue operation was immense. Because Caracas was more than 1,000 miles away, the helicopter coming to pick the expedition up needed a DC-3 plane flying with it to carry extra fuel. For the helicopter to land in the jungle, the Indians had to chop down enough trees to clear a small helicopter pad.

When the helicopter finally landed, Monique Delmasso was immediately put on board and attended to by a doctor. The Indians, who had no intention of setting foot inside something as unfamiliar as a helicopter, were given enough food to make it back home. Kiké got on board. Finally, the helicopter swooped up and plucked the four climbers from their dangerous perch. "And we just helicoptered back to civilization," Todd says.

As they flew away, Todd looked back at Mount Aritityope. Although he could appreciate the mountain's beauty as he watched it fade, he would never forget the desperation of hanging on the face and looking for parachutes he would never see. Still, he kept looking back. It wasn't until they were almost 100 miles away that Todd lost sight of the shark's fin jutting so gloriously above the jungle. Like the Yanamani had pointed out before, the mist around the mountain was now blue.

When they got back to the United States, Todd and Paul began preparing for their next climb. It will be in Pakistan, in a remote glacier in the Himalaya Mountains.

Monique Delmasso recovered from her malnutrition. However, she was barely able to climb for a year.

Kiké Arnal, Rick Ridgeway, and the rest of the expedition are alive and well.

To this day, the parachutes have never been found.

The Toughest Race on Earth

Team American Pride's Quest to Conquer the Raid Gauloises

1 * Bungle in the Jungle

Team American Pride's Pat Harwood brought his machete *{ma-SHET-ee}* down hard on the thick, green vine staring him in the face. He was trying to clear a path through jungle so thick that he couldn't see 10 feet ahead. The machete's long, curved blade, which had once been razor-sharp, was now dull. But with his five-person team lost somewhere in the jungle of a wild island called

Michael (in front) and the other members of the 1992 Team American Pride slogged through mountain canyons in one grueling stage of the Raid Gauloises in Oman.

NATHAN BILOW

Borneo, Pat had no choice but to keep trying.

As Pat kept chopping, the other members of Team American Pride (TAP), stood behind him, studying a topographical map and looking miserable. The five of them, including Bruce Schliemann *{SHLEE-man}*, Rick Holman, Mark Burnett, and Cathy Sassin-Smith, were totally lost. They were so lost that they had been hiking in circles through the jungle for almost an entire day and night. Their feet hurt and they were sweating a lot because Borneo, in Southeast Asia, is located on the equator, which is the hottest part of the world. Although they didn't say it, they were all probably thinking the same thing: We're never going to win this crazy race.

Race? In the jungle? That's right. Team American Pride was one of 40 teams competing in the Raid Gauloises *{gal-WAZ}*. Held each year in a different exotic country, the Raid challenges five-person teams to race in five different events almost without stopping for up to 10 days and nights. They race through jungles, deserts, mountains, oceans — whatever each country has to offer.

The starting line of the 1994 Raid was in a small village in Borneo called Ba Kelalan *{Bah Kell-lah-LAN}* From there, the teams would race almost 300 miles through the jungle to a place called Mulu. The only reason they would stop was if they needed to eat or sleep. And even then they wouldn't stop for very long: Most teams would sleep for only a few hours a night!

In the first event of this Raid, teams would hike through the jungle for almost 80 miles. Then, they

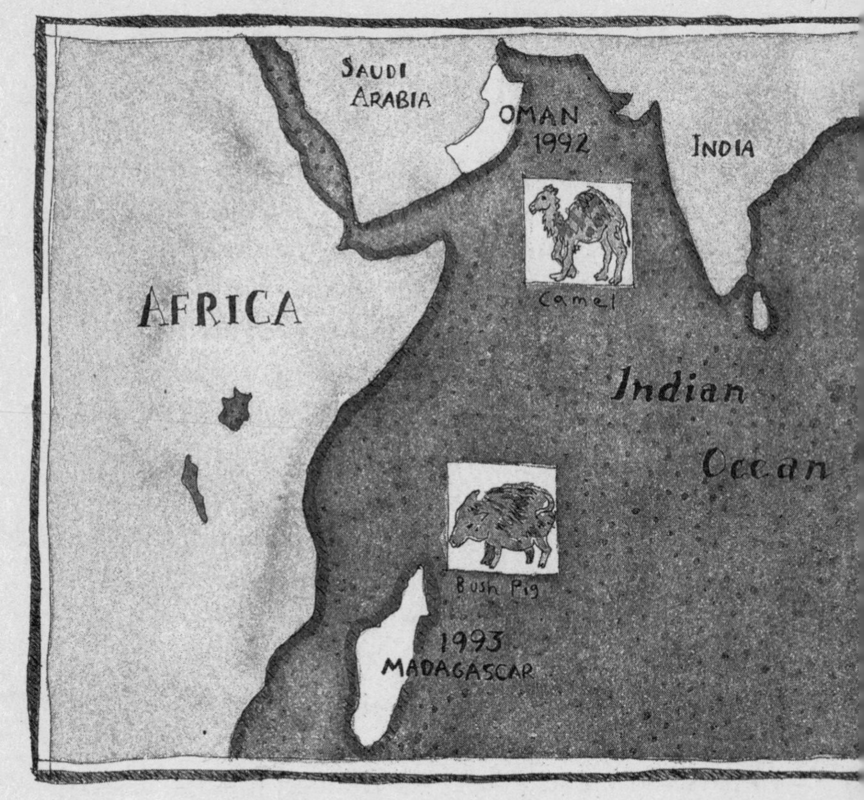

would paddle canoes for 20 miles down the Kubaan River, then raft 40 miles down a faster river called the Tutoh *{TOO-toe}*. Then they'd jump on mountain bikes and pedal through the jungle for 50 miles. The teams next had to navigate through caves, walking underground for almost 30 miles, before canoeing another 10 miles to the finish line.

No wonder people call the Raid Gauloises "The Toughest Race on Earth." Ever since a French radio journalist named Gerard Fusil held the first Raid Gauloises

in New Zealand in 1989, teams from around the world have come to try his unusual event, even though not all of them finish. And that's the way it is supposed to be. "The goal of the Raid," Gerard says often, meaning every word, "is to push individuals to their mental, physical, and emotional limits. If they cannot push themselves that far, then they will not be able to finish."

The events are different every year. For instance, the 1993 Raid, which was held on the island of Madagascar, featured skydiving, mountain climbing, whitewater canoeing, desert hiking, and ocean kayaking. The 1992 Raid in Oman included both camel riding and horseback riding. In 1991, in the Central American country of Costa Rica, contestants used local dugout canoes for one event. In New Caledonia, an island in the Pacific east of Australia, there was catamaran sailboat racing in 1990.

Borneo looked like it would be the toughest challenge of all. In addition to simple things like overwhelming heat and humidity, there would be difficult terrain, and insects and wild animals — leopards, crocodiles, poisonous centipedes, and lots of snakes.

As tough as the jungle is, though, the hardest part of the Raid Gauloises takes place inside the people racing. It's a long, hard race and it punishes the body with effort and fatigue. After awhile, competitors get so tired that all they want to do is quit. They think about going home and sleeping in their nice warm beds instead of in the wet jungle. They dream of taking hot showers or eating big plates of hot food!

Race officials set up certain spots along the course called checkpoints. There, the officials check in each team so they can keep track of everyone, and know how each team is doing against the competition.

As the members of Team American Pride trudged through the jungle, they tried not to get discouraged. It was hard, though. It seemed that the more they walked, the more lost they became. "I had flown halfway around the world to win the Raid Gauloises, and I realized it might not happen," Mark said later. "I began to wonder what was the use of going on."

Finally, after more than 30 hours of looking, the team found the trail it was searching for. But later on, when the five of them arrived at the first checkpoint, they got bad news: they were in last place. The other teams were almost a whole day ahead. Team American Pride had to face the hard fact that its plans to win the whole race might not come off. But in the back of some team members' minds was the question: Could we maybe, if we try really hard, come back and win this thing?

2 * Great Expectations

Mark Burnett first read about the Raid Gauloises in 1990. Opening up the *The Los Angeles Times* one Sunday morning, he was intrigued by an article about an obscure French endurance race in Costa Rica. "I couldn't believe there was actually a race through a place filled with alligators, poisonous snakes, and panthers," he recalls. "And the thought that the race lasted almost eleven days — incredible!"

Mark looked across the breakfast table at his wife, Dianne. He was very excited.

"I must do this race!" he exclaimed. Without having to say so, she believed him. Mark had a way of making difficult things seem easy. When he was growing up in London, England, he was very poor. Yet by the time he was 28, having moved to the U.S. just six years before, he had become financially successful in the credit card business. If Mark said he was going to race through the jungle for 10 days and nights, then Dianne knew it would happen.

Immediately, Mark got up from the table and wrote a letter to the people in Paris who organize the Raid. He wanted to know how to enter. He mailed it, and then waited. One day, the phone rang. It was a man named Gerard Fusil calling from Paris. He told Mark that if he wanted to enter the Raid, he needed to be part of a team. There had to be five people on the team, and at least one had to be a woman. He told Mark that the next Raid Gauloises would take place in 10 more months. It would be held in a small country in the Middle East called Oman, which was next to Saudi Arabia. Contestants would be asked to ride horseback, mountain climb, kayak in the sea, canyon (which is basically climbing down mountains), and even ride camels. Gerard also pointed out that no team from the U.S. had ever competed before.

"I'll be there," Mark told Gerard confidently.

Despite the Raid's dangers, Mark had no problem finding three adventurous people for his team. He found them working out at his gym. There was an aerobics instructor named Michael Carson, an actor named Owen Rutledge, and a stockbroker named Norman Archer Hunte. All of them lifted weights and ran often, so Mark believed they were the right people for his team. The team was coming together, but still needed a woman member.

Mark picked up the phone and called Gerard in Paris. "Do you know of any women who might be interested in joining our team?" he asked.

"Why, yes," Gerard answered. "I just got a letter today from a woman who lives near Los Angeles. Why don't you give her a call?"

The woman's name was Susan Hemond. She worked in television and had grown up in a family involved with professional baseball. In college, Susan ran track. Afterward, she began to look for a sport in which she could compete alongside men. She tried sailing, she tried running, but nothing really caught her interest. It was only when she read the same article in *The Los Angeles Times* that Mark had read that Susan knew she had finally found her sport. She got Mark's number from the organizers and called him. When Mark asked her to join, Susan didn't have to think twice. "Yes!" she replied, almost shouting into the phone.

Mark decided to name the team after his adopted country, and with that, Team American Pride was born. The five teammates began intense physical training right away. They ran and lifted weights. On weekends, they took classes in rock climbing, horseback riding, and kayaking. The special training paid off. Within six months, they were able to climb even the biggest rocks without difficulty.

To learn more about Oman, Mark spent his spare time studying at the library. Like neighboring Saudi Arabia, parts of Oman are made up of desert. But Mark also discovered that a vast mountain range known as Jebel Akdar runs like a spine through the northern part of Oman. The Jebel is home to lions, snakes, and wolves. With a shudder, Mark realized that Team American Pride would soon be spending many days and nights in the middle of those fierce mountains. And because Raid rules state that teams cannot carry weapons, he knew they would have to be very cautious.

The 10 months passed quickly. As he sat on the plane taking the team to Oman, Mark thought of how quickly his life had changed. He'd gone from an average guy reading his Sunday newspaper to a competitor who would race through the wilderness with the toughest, most adventurous athletes in the world. Would he be up to the test? Would the team? His biggest fear was that mentally he might not be strong enough when the going got tough.

"I will not quit," he vowed. It sounded more like a prayer. "I will not quit."

3 * SWAMPED

It was 5:30 in the morning when a rifle shot signaled the start of the 1992 Raid Gauloises. In the predawn chill, American Pride and 50 other teams charged up a washed-out creek bed atop bareback horses. They would gallop 30 miles before dismounting to begin 100 miles of climbing and running through the Jebel Akdar mountains. The air was filled with dust and confusion. Teams jockeyed for position and tried not to lose each other in the crowd. "It was incredibly exciting," Susan said later. "I couldn't believe we were finally starting the Raid Gauloises. It was like a dream come true."

The order of events had been announced at a pre-race briefing just two days before: horseback riding, mountain climbing, canyoning, mountain climbing (again), sea kayaking, climbing, canyoning (again), and then camel riding. Teams were cautioned to carry plenty of food and water.

In the first event, the team leaders selected the horses, and Team American Pride ended up with one bad horse that was too old to keep up. The team members ended up having to walk the horse instead of having it carry one of them. Still, Team American Pride kept its spirits up. Even when TAP finished the horseback riding six hours behind the lead teams, it worked as a unit. But that didn't last.

The initial climb into the mountains through Snake Canyon involved going through a waterfall. "We were soaked," Susan remembers with a shiver. "I was totally freezing." Mark watched with dismay as his teammates stopped cooperating and focused on their own misery.

At the top of the waterfall, Owen refused to go on until the team dried its clothing by the fire at the checkpoint. He was afraid that his cold, wet socks might cause blisters. There was an argument. Susan felt it was important to go on. No other team had stopped to dry its clothes, she emphasized. If TAP stopped now, it would fall further and further behind. But Owen refused to listen. He sat down and began to dry his clothes. "I knew right then and there that we were in trouble," Mark observed. Unable to go on without Owen, they stopped.

It got worse. The next day, Mark's lack of experience with the compass and the complexity of the directions got them lost. They walked around in circles for hours before finding the right trail. In the meantime, they ran low on water. When just a swallow of water remained in the team canteen, they were desperate: Whenever they got thirsty, they passed around the team canteen. But instead of swallowing the water, they swished it around their mouths, then spit it back into the canteen and passed it to the next person.

The journey through the mountains that should have lasted two days stretched on to three, then four for Team American Pride. Susan felt the first twinges of what was later diagnosed as a bad bacterial infection. (By the end of the race, she would lose 20 pounds and require medical treatment.) Team American Pride fell more than 24 hours behind the leaders.

When they reached the Arabian Sea to begin 100 miles of sea kayaking, the team members knew they would have to do something drastic in order to win. Watching a storm blow in dark and fierce from the East, they decided on a plan. They knew that they were stronger paddlers than the others, so they thought if they pushed through to the end of the kayaking without sleep, they could get into the lead.

Under black skies, Team American Pride slipped into the kayaks and pushed off. Mark and Michael shared a two-person boat, as did Susan and Norman. Owen, who was the strongest paddler, had his own. Bravely, they paddled out through six-foot breaking waves.

"The waves were so huge that the stern of my kayak was pointing straight up in the sky as we crested the top of them," Susan says, shaking her head in wonder. "I was facing straight down the back of the wave." They turned parallel to the coast 300 yards offshore. Digging their paddles in the surf, they raced as hard as they could.

The storm hit. Raging wind forced rain through their clothing, soaking them. Sharks circled their boats. Rescue helicopters swooped low as they headed out to pull troubled teams out of the sea. Undaunted, Team American Pride pushed on. "We were really moving," Mark says proudly.

Then Owen made it clear that he wasn't going on. In fact, he was giving up and paddling in to the rocky shore. His teammates could tell that his boat was likely to get smashed to pieces on the rocks. Everyone was screaming at Owen to stay, but he headed for shore. His teammates hoped he just needed to be alone, but he never came back. He survived the trip in. However, without all five members, it was no longer a team. In effect, the moment Owen left, Team American Pride was disqualified. Angrily, the remaining teammates dug their paddles into the water. But they went slower now, knowing their efforts didn't matter.

The stern is the name for the back of a boat. The front of a boat is called the bow, which rhymes with wow.

A day before the finish, Michael severely injured ligaments in his ankle, and had to drop out. But making good on his vow, Mark didn't quit. Susan, Norman, and he went on to finish the 1992 Raid Gauloises in 10 days, 1 hour, and 15 minutes. They were 39th out of 51 teams, but since the team was incomplete, they didn't officially finish. In 10 short months, though, Team American Pride had seen the Raid go from dream to reality. For Mark, that wasn't enough anymore. "As good as I felt about crossing the finish line — about having actually completed the Raid Gauloises, something very few people would dream of attempting — I wasn't satisfied. I knew I had to come back and try to win."

On the plane going home, Mark and his wife were talking about the team. Mark knew he needed to make drastic changes. No more dreamers from the local gym. For the 1993 Raid Gauloises in Madagascar, Mark wanted the best of the best on Team American Pride. For 1993, Mark thought with a grin, I want Navy SEALS.

4 * New Respect

At first glance, Bruce Schliemann, Rick Holman, and Pat Harwood don't look like commandos. Bruce, 31, is long and lean, built like a professional cyclist. Rick, 34, has a mustache and is very quiet. Pat, 33, with straight blond hair and a beach boy smile, looks like a lifeguard. But the three are all Navy SEALS (the name comes from Sea, Air, Land — signifying their ability to do battle in all three). Every day they do hours of push-ups, sit-ups, and running to stay in top physical condition. They are trained in the martial arts, deep-sea diving, and jungle warfare. Perhaps most important, they are trained to be team players. Every SEAL knows that in battle, his teammate might save his life, so they all learn to trust and rely on each other.

Mark Burnett had learned all this about the SEALS from the movie *Navy SEALS*, and he knew they were perfect for Team American Pride. Still, Mark was nervous about approaching them. He thought they would be grim, hostile, and probably mean.

He was wrong.

The three SEALS peppered Mark with questions about the race, and Mark found them easy to talk to. After he answered all their questions, the three Navy men said, "We want to do it." Fortunately, the Navy thought it was a good idea, too, and gave them extra time off to train.

Once the SEALS joined the team, Mark decided to ask Susan to be the woman member again. She had proven how tough she was in Oman. "I didn't walk away from the Raid in Oman feeling like I had done all I needed to do," Susan explained. "I really felt like I had to go back."

The new Team American Pride began practicing right away. Because the events change every year at the Raid to fit in with each country's features, the participants need to learn new skills. The Raid in Madagascar featured skydiving, whitewater canoeing, mountain climbing, desert hiking, and ocean kayaking.

When Mark wondered where they would learn to skydive, he found out that the SEALS each had parachuted out of airplanes several hundred times and were instructors. That's when Mark knew just how wonderful having the SEALS on his team could be. Even though Mark was very nervous about learning to jump out of a plane, he knew the SEALS would help him overcome that. For the six months that they trained together, they taught him and Susan how to be tougher, smarter, and have more stamina than he ever dreamed.

When the team took its place on the starting line in Madagascar, Mark was very nervous. But looking at Pat, Rick, Bruce, and Susan, he felt that he was part of a great team. "These SEALS are real pros," he thought to himself. He was comforted to be part of such a professional group.

Team American Pride took the lead right away. The five teammates parachuted together and settled to earth in perfect formation in the middle of the landing zone. While other teams struggled with their parachutes, the Americans quickly took theirs off and changed into the clothes they would wear for the next 10 days: Running shoes, T-shirts, long pants, backpacks filled with food and water, and wide-brimmed hats to protect them from the sun.

They would need all the protection they could get. The temperature was 135 degrees on the hot Madagascan plains. Topping off their canteens, they began marching into the Makay Massif mountain range, an area like America's Grand Canyon, where they would spend the next four days.

Within hours, however, Mark was having trouble in

the heat. He felt dizzy. He was thirstier than he had ever been in his life. He slumped to the ground, exhausted. Nobody said anything as they waited for him to get up. Then Bruce gently lifted Mark's pack off of his back. He slipped it on his own back, so that he was carrying two packs. "Thanks," Mark mumbled, rising to his feet and starting to march again.

"You don't have to thank me," Bruce said, trying to lift Mark's spirits. He could see that his teammate was discouraged and embarrassed. "You might have to carry my pack next time."

On and on they marched. Rick navigated flawlessly as they moved from the flat plains into the towering canyons of the Makay. The blinding heat of daytime gave way to cold thunderstorms at night, but they didn't stop to sleep. They climbed up and down huge rock walls in the wet darkness. When their water ran out, they refilled their bottles from swamps, making sure to add special tablets to kill any germs.

Water is very important to a body. People can survive without food for more than two months, but can survive without water for only about a week.

After four days, the team was in fifth place, but was running out of water. The next river was at least a day's march ahead. After studying the map, Pat suggested going off the route onto an old riverbed in hopes of finding some. The day was hot and everybody was sweating a lot. Nobody wanted to detour, especially in the heat, but they knew there was no other way.

As the team headed for the riverbed, Bruce suddenly fainted. Pat splashed some water on him. Bruce came to and rose to his feet. "Sorry," he said with a weak smile, and reached for his pack. But Mark's hand was already there.

"Let me take it," Mark said.

"You're sure?" Bruce replied. He felt better, but not totally.

"I'm sure." At last, Mark knew he belonged on the same team as the SEALS. Although they had much more training in these areas than he did, he knew he could help them out, too, when needed.

The team pressed on. At the start of the last event, sea kayaking, the Americans were in 13th place. If they hadn't been forced to go off the trail for water that one day, they might have been in the lead. They took stock of their situation. None of them had slept in more than three days. But they decided their goal would be to push themselves to the limit.

As one, the team pushed into the placid waters of the bay. It was 5:05 a.m. The tide had just come in. It was still cool because the sun hadn't come up yet. They didn't talk as they paddled smoothly down the coast. They were too tired for that. Smoothly, efficiently, they paddled mile after mile after mile. They moved up a few places. The lead team, a crew of French Alpine guides named Jura, was only 10 hours ahead. Team American Pride's strong bodies were breaking, but still they pushed on.

They moved up to sixth. The finish line was just 50 miles off. By then, nobody had slept for four days. Some team members were actually paddling in their sleep at times.

Fifth place. The fatigue grew worse. "It got so bad, I was falling asleep in my boat," Pat recalls. "People couldn't concentrate. I was screaming to keep myself awake." Finally, their bodies broke. They had to stop and sleep. And if they couldn't go on, they couldn't win. After slipping to the beach for a nap, Team American Pride eventually went on to finish the 1993 Raid Gauloises in ninth place. Its finishing time was nine days and eight hours, more than a full day faster than in Oman.

Pat looked at Mark as they got out of the kayaks. "Where's next year's race?" he asked.

"Borneo."

"We're coming back," Pat stated flatly. The others overheard. They looked at Pat. They seemed to know what he was about to say, and to agree with it. "We're coming back next year and we're gonna win, make no mistake about it."

5 * Perseverance

Before going to Madagascar, Susan had been told by her doctor that she risked lasting damage to her body if she ever did the Raid again. Though she went anyway, she decided to retire at the finish line. So despite its drive to win, the team put off serious training for Borneo until a replacement for Susan could be found. In May, just five months before the Raid, a new woman joined Team American Pride. Her name was Cathy Sassin-Smith. Cathy was a bodybuilder and a runner who sometimes appeared on the television show, *American Gladiators*. In addition, her view of life was optimistic, always looking for the good in people and events. That would be very important in Borneo, especially if the team ran into tough times. And though everyone was sad that Susan was no longer a part of the team, they soon found Cathy to be a good addition. By the time they left for Borneo in October, Pat, Mark, Rick, and Bruce were treating Cathy like a sister.

When the team got to Borneo, they noticed that the other teams were treating them differently than they had the year before. It was almost as though they were afraid of Team American Pride. "I couldn't figure out why," said Bruce, "then it hit me: We were among the favorites to win. Before, nobody took us seriously enough to be scared. But now that we were capable of winning, teams kept their distance from us."

The night before the Raid began, Team American Pride sat down to plot strategy. Each of them agreed that winning was the reason they were there. "I think the first leg [jungle navigation] will be the easiest," Pat pointed out, "so we should push as hard as we can. If we can be either in the lead or close to the lead when we get to the canoes, I think we can take it."

The others agreed. The jungle navigation leg looked

hilly and dense, but they saw no reason to be worried about it. The members of the team took a good hard look at each other. They were as fit as they could possibly be. Their muscles were hard and their minds were ready. Although the other teams were very good, American Pride knew that it was better. "Let's get out there and do it," Pat said, trying not to sound as nervous as he felt. His teammates nodded — they were ready.

The race began the next day at noon, with the hot sun burning down on the competitors. Team American Pride charged away from the starting line, eager to set the pace. But as soon as the five Americans stepped into the jungle, they ran into trouble. Through a simple map-reading error, they got so lost that they wandered around in circles for a whole day, trying to find the right trail. The course guide book, which described in very fine detail what type of trails the teams would be traveling on, had originally been written in French. It had not been translated into English correctly. So while French teams knew to look for a very wide dirt road, the Americans were reading a translation that told them to look for a "forest trail." Other English-speaking teams were not affected by the translation because they were following other teams. TAP, in its push to win, broke off on its own.

"We were looking for a skinny little path, not a big road," Rick said later. "In fact, we were actually on the right road for a long time, but we kept saying that it couldn't possibly be the right one because it was too big."

After frustrating hours walking back and forth in the jungle, Team American Pride members decided it was time to take matters into their own hands. They would cut their own path, no matter how thick the jungle was.

"We know where we are, and where we have to go," Rick pointed out, holding up a map and compass. "So let's do it."

Because TAP carried only one machete, the work was slow. Mile after mile the team members chopped their way into the thick vegetation. They were almost too exhausted to talk. But worst of all, they knew their chances of winning were slipping away. By the time they got back on track, the team members were so demoralized that they had to have a team meeting. Mark had become disenchanted. He had diarrhea and felt terrible; he knew they had no hope of winning.

Pat started the meeting off. "What should we do, should we go on, even though we're not going to win, or should we quit?" The word "quit" stung them. Even thinking about quitting went against everything they believed in. Rick was the one who broke the silence. "QUIT?" he said as if he'd been insulted. He was the quietest member of the team and only spoke if he had something important to say. So when Rick made quitting sound like it was the most awful thing they could do, everybody listened closely. He only said that one word, but he spoke it so forcefully that it was like a slap in the face to the team.

"He's right," Pat said, a smile spreading slowly across

his face. "We can't quit. OK, so we might not win, but that's not the most important thing anymore. The important thing is that we're here representing America. If we quit, people are going to think that Americans are quitters."

The rest of the team nodded in agreement. "It's gonna get even tougher out there," Bruce added, getting to his feet. He reached for his backpack and slowly slid it on. "No matter what, Team American Pride has to finish this race." He was thinking something else, too: Maybe we can still win this thing.

So they continued on. Mile after mile they kept walking, telling bad jokes to keep their spirits up. Bruce set the pace, keeping it fast. Most of the team members felt very optimistic. They felt they could close the gap with the leaders. But Mark was still very discouraged and felt they would never make any headway. TAP faced a second tough night in the jungle, but pushed on without sleep. "It was scary in there," Pat pointed out later. "We never saw any animals or snakes, but every time we'd shine our lights off the trail and into the jungle, we could see the reflections of their eyes looking out at us."

On the morning of the third day, Bruce, who had been walking ahead to check the trail, felt his knee give out while he was climbing down a piece of wet rock. He fell, and the pain was so intense that he could barely stand up. Somehow he did, but it was not without a struggle. His face was twisted with pain. "You OK, man?" Pat asked with concern.

"Yeah," Bruce said through clenched teeth. "I'm fine." He followed Pat down the trail in the pouring rain.

But less than a mile later, Bruce's knee gave out again. Slowly, he fought to stand up. He willed himself to go forward and keep pace with the team.

And then it happened again. This time the pain was so bad that Bruce could barely walk. "I'm smoked, guys," Bruce said, using a SEAL term that means totally wiped out. "I gotta stop."

Sadly, the other members of the team shook hands with Bruce and walked on. He knew that when they got to the next village, they would radio for a helicopter to come pick him up.

After Bruce's departure, Mark's resolve to continue grew weaker and weaker. He knew that everybody who did the Raid had moments where they wanted to quit. He also knew that whenever he felt like quitting, the best thing he could do was to think of something else. But when he tried to think of something else, the only thing he could think about was being home with his family. "I've done this twice before, I have nothing to prove," he thought glumly. "My body hurts all over. I'm totally miserable. We're not going to win, and if we cross the finish line in last place, people are going to laugh at us. Why should I keep going?"

Mark thought his feelings might change once the team started the canoeing stage, but he still felt low. So as the team fought its way down the Kubaan, a muddy, frothy river filled with crocodiles and monitor lizards,

Mark began to feel more miserable than ever. He didn't want to do this anymore. "As far as I was concerned, I hadn't come for the race or the experience," Mark said. "I had come to win, and from the onset, it was a disaster."

Soon Mark began having trouble concentrating on paddling. He could tell that he was probably hurting the team more than helping it. So when he and his teammates got out of the canoes to start the rafting, Mark pulled everyone aside. "Look, I've done this twice before," he stated. "I don't need to get kicked in the shins to know that it hurts. I'm not going on."

Pat, Rick, and Cathy were shocked. "Mark," Cathy pleaded, "you've got to at least try. Does a football team quit just beause they're behind at halftime?" Mark looked at Cathy, too numb and tired to care anymore. The Raid Gauloises had finally proven too tough for him.

When the rafting leg began, Mark was standing on the shore, watching them paddle away. He knew in his heart that he wasn't a quitter. He thought of what Gerard Fusil had told him a long time before about the Raid. That it was designed to take people to their "mental, physical, and emotional limits." Mark knew that he had finally reached that point. He wished he hadn't quit, but he knew that he couldn't go on, either.

Pat, Rick, and Cathy pushed on. They hadn't told Mark, but they felt like quitting sometimes, too. "Mark had to do what he had to do," Pat said with a shrug of the shoulders. "That's the way the Raid is. It's designed to break you, and sometimes it does."

Pat, Rick, and Cathy made it through the rafting leg without too much trouble. Things got very tough, however, on the mountain biking leg. The course was on steep, rolling mountain roads. On the downhills, which sometimes lasted for two or three miles, they went as fast as 60 miles per hour! But the uphills were just as long, and were so difficult that they had to push their bikes all the way to the top in the punishing heat.

After the heat and the hills, the Mulu Caves seemed easy to Rick, Cathy, and Pat. Wearing miner's headlamps, they walked through the world-famous caves, stopping sometimes to shine their lights up to the ceiling where a huge colony of bats lived.

Once through the caves, Rick, Pat, and Cathy crossed the finish line. Mark and Bruce were waiting for them, and the whole team celebrated together. "It's OK that we didn't win, it really is," Pat said. "Hey, we gave it our best shot. The important thing is that we came and did something really, really tough. I still believe we would have done well if we hadn't got lost that first day."

The members of the team looked at each other. They were all thinking the same thought. "There's always next year," Pat said with a grin. As he had in Madagascar the year before, he was saying the words that were on their minds. "There's no doubt Team American Pride has what it takes to win the Raid Gauloises. Just because we fail once doesn't mean we're not going to try again. In fact, we'll keep trying until we do win."

Siberian Express

A Wild Ride Down a Raging Russian River

1 * Light at the End of the Tunnel

When kayaking expert Beth Rypins *{rip-pins}* went to Russia in the summer of 1993, all she wanted was peace and quiet. And big rapids to ride her kayak on, of course. But that was all, nothing more. She didn't want any stress or worries, because she'd had enough of that all spring. She simply wanted to spend a low-key summer paddling her kayak through the biggest, most untamed white water rapids she could find. It would be relaxing.

Of course, it didn't work out like that.

"In June I had just graduated from university with a degree in Soviet politics," Beth, 31, says, starting the story. She talks quickly, as if hurrying to get all the words out before she forgets what she wants to say. "All during the spring, I was really busy with studying in the library and taking tests. By the time I was finished with all of that, I was really tired of being around books and school. All I wanted to do was go kayaking."

A kayak is a very thin boat that is just wide enough for one person to sit in. It looks like a canoe, but skinnier and shorter. The paddler sits inside, surrounded by a "skirt" that covers the opening and keeps the water out. The front and back ends narrow down to a point. That is so the kayak can slice through water quickly and easily. If the ends were wide and flat, the water would push against the boat and slow it down.

Beth has kayaked for fun ever since she took her first paddling class at age 15. She didn't have any money, so she cooked a pan of brownies and traded them for lessons at the Sierra Kayak School. The school is on the south fork of the American River, not too far from her hometown of San Francisco, but located between Sacramento, California and Reno, Nevada. "I got hooked right away," she says with a laugh. Beth laughs a lot. It's a hearty, happy laugh, the kind made by someone who spends a lot of time outdoors and never has to worry about laughing too loud. "For the next ten years I ate, slept, and breathed kayaking," she says. "It was all-consuming."

LARS HOLBEK

Beth Rypins went down Siberia's Sumulta River in a kayak (see book's back cover), but her Russian friends used rafts that carried more people.

Along the way, Beth learned that white water kayaking (the term "white water" comes from the color that river water gets when it moves very fast) isn't just floating a boat down a river. It is a combination of competing with the river, and working with it, all at the same time. The object is to go through the rapids (parts of rivers where the water moves quickly and which often have rocks breaking through the surface), riding the kayak wherever the river goes. This is called "running" the rapids. Following the river means that sometimes you fly off the edge of waterfalls!

Good paddlers learn to "read" the water, searching for

RUSSIA
Barnaul
Gorno-Altaysk
Sumulta River
ALTAI MTS.
MONGOLIA
CHINA
N

the best path through even the biggest rapids. They learn what water looks like as it flows over and around things like rocks and trees that lurk under the water — and how to steer away from them. The best paddlers learn to stay calm even when the water gets so fast that the boat feels out of control.

It's not easy, though. When calm river water starts going fast enough to become white water, it begins to buck and snort like a rodeo bull. It can pitch kayaks up and down and side to side without mercy. Paddlers can be tossed out of their boats and into the water.

Beth fell out of her kayak a lot at first. Most of the time, it was because she took too many chances. She didn't know enough to respect the awesome power of rivers. She didn't know that big rapids can pull a person underwater and keep them under until they drown. She didn't know that white water can destroy boats, and the people in them, by pounding them into rocks. But after more than a few dunks in very scary rapids, she learned.

"For years when I was starting, I was aggressive and didn't know the dangers," she says. "I took horrible swims in big rapids, but I didn't know enough to be scared. Now I'm adamant about not paddling in a situation where I'm in over my head."

The more Beth practiced, the better she got. After she finished high school, she decided to pursue river-running as an occupation instead of going right to college. In the summers, she worked as a raft guide on the American River. During the winter, she used the money she made to travel to other parts of the world to kayak. On one trip to South America, she paddled from 10,000 feet up in the Andes Mountains down to almost sea level. And in a 1989 trip that eventually changed her life, she traveled to Siberia, in Russia, with a group called Project RAFT (Russians and Americans For Teamwork).

The Andes Mountains [AN-dees] run down the western side of South America from Panama to the Strait of Magellan, a narrow passage of water between Argentina and Chile.

"People from all over Russia were there," Beth says. "The thing that I remember most about it was that even though it was early spring and super, super, super cold, the warmth of the people shone through."

One of the things that made the trip so memorable had to do with the period of time in which Beth grew up. In the years between about 1948 and 1989, the United States and Russia were engaged in a military standoff that was known as the Cold War. During that time, Americans lived with the fear that nuclear war with Russia could erupt at any time. Those feelings affected Beth and her fellow travelers.

"I had been brought up to fear Russians," Beth says. "I thought they were these tough, emotionless people — and on the surface they were. But underneath I found them to be curious and intriguing. Suddenly, all the propaganda I learned growing up didn't make sense."

When Beth came back to the U.S., she decided she

wanted to learn as much about the Russian people and their political history as she could. When she started college in the fall of 1990, she chose to study Soviet politics and history. She even learned to speak their language, which is very different from English and has its own alphabet.

Though the studying was hard, Beth was determined to learn all she could. The school she attended, the University of California at Berkeley, is one of the best in the country and she knew she was learning a lot. In the winter of her last year there, Beth could see the light at the end of the tunnel: Only a few more months until graduation. It looked like the final few months would be easy. When it's all over, Beth thought, I'll go back to Russia and spend a relaxing summer kayaking and speaking Russian.

Then something terrible happened. On May 6, 1993, Jaroslav Mach *{mock}*, a very close friend of Beth's and one of the world's best-known white water experts, was kayaking on the Eel River in northern California. His boat got pinned amid some rocks and the water rushed over him. Unable to lift his head above the raging current, he drowned. The loss had a real effect on Beth: It scared her. She began to think that maybe someday *she* would die on a river, too. But Beth chose to turn the experience around and use it to strengthen herself.

"That situation made me realize that fear has a lot of power behind it," she says now. "It can turn any situation from positive to negative. If you can control fear, like I chose to do, it can be a good thing. I actually got more power from fear after that."

When she finally went through graduation exercises, Beth was mentally and physically exhausted. Still, she couldn't wait to get to Russia and start kayaking on the river.

Beth thought the trip might be more fun if some friends came, too. So she asked two kayakers, her boyfriend, Lars Holbek, who is a world-class paddler, and her good friend, Renee Goddard, to join her. She also invited another good friend, a San Francisco firefighter named Caroline Paul, to make the trip. Also, a whole group of Russians from the 1989 Project RAFT would be waiting for them at the river. "I can't wait to be in a beautiful place," she told Lars as she threw her clothes in the big backpack she uses for a suitcase. "This trip is going to be so laid back."

2 * SHOTGUN DIPLOMACY

The river Beth decided to kayak was called the Sumulta. It is located in the Altai Mountains, which lie in the area where the countries of Russia, China, and Mongolia meet. The river is very remote, and nobody had ever paddled its upper reaches before.

Beth and her group entered Russia in a small port called Sochi. If you look at a map of Russia, Sochi is located on the eastern side of the Black Sea. Moscow, Russia's capital city, lies 900 miles due north. "Sochi is a long way from civilization," Beth notes dryly.

But none of that mattered as Beth arrived. After months and months of waiting, she was finally in Russia! She felt wonderful and happy, especially when two Russian friends, Vanya and Oleg, joined them.

The happiness didn't last for very long. As Beth and her group arrived, they were confronted by local policemen. "Come with us," the police commanded.

They were led into a small room, where a large man joined them. His face was unshaven and his clothes smelled like he hadn't taken a bath in a week. Gruffly, he told the Americans to sit down. One at a time, he questioned them about why they wanted to come to Russia. He searched their bags to make sure nobody carried guns or drugs. Even while he was looking through their belongings, he continued to ask them the same questions over and over. "Why do you want to come to Russia? Do you have any valuables in your bags that you have not told us about? How long will you be staying here?"

The scary ordeal dragged on for over an hour. Just when Beth was beginning to wonder if the man was going to accuse them of being spies or smugglers, and throw them into jail, he let them go. Before he could change his mind, Beth and her companions raced to the Sochi airport to catch the plane that would fly them 2,500 miles to the town of Barnaul, from which they would take other means of transportation to another town. From there, they would hike to the Sumulta River. If they missed the plane, they would have to wait a week before the next one was scheduled to come.

They made it. Actually, they didn't have to hurry, after all. The Sochi Airport had run out of fuel for the airplanes. Beth's heart sank when she found out they might have to wait for days until some could be found. "This is ridiculous," Beth said to Lars. She was getting frustrated. "All I want is to go kayaking," she said. "That's all. Why does everything seem to be going wrong?"

It turned out to be not so bad. After less than a day, fuel was found and the plane took off. Looking out the window, Beth could see Russia unfolding below her. It was wide-open and untamed. There were no cities and few villages. As they got closer to the Sumulta River, she was able to see huge mountains and thick green forests.

"I'm really excited about getting on the water," Beth whispered to Lars. She also was eager to learn whether or not the kayaks and equipment she had shipped ahead were waiting for them at the river. She hoped nothing was damaged.

The plane landed in the town of Barnaul. From there, Vanya and Oleg would show them how to get to the Sumulta River. Beth and her friends took a train (it was very old and slow), then a bus (even older and slower), then yet another bus (so old and slow that it barely moved) until they were finally in the small town of Gorno-Altaysk. They got off and looked around. The Altai Mountains loomed high above the town. The rugged range reached to the clouds. Even in the middle of the summer, they had snow on them. The Sumulta was on the other side of the mountains. It was going to be quite a hike.

Beth and her friends bought enough food for four or five days and began hiking into the mountains. They had picked up a map, though they had some doubts about it. Beth had learned on her last trip that Russian maps weren't very good. Still, they followed the direction that the map said they should go. "We hiked for an entire day in the wrong direction," Beth recalls with disgust. "It wasn't until we ran into a local citizen that we found out the right way to go. We turned around, and basically discovered that we had to hike straight up the side of the mountain."

The trail was muddy and extremely steep. The six paddlers climbed and climbed. Then, at the end of the first day, they heard a funny noise. Beth turned toward the noise and couldn't believe what she saw. It was a tractor stopping to give them a lift. "These five happy, farmer-renegade types were driving their four-wheel drive tractor to the other side of the mountain. They looked dirty and ragged, but we didn't care. We were just happy to have the ride."

When Beth and the others hopped onto the tractor's trailer, right away they noticed two things that made them worry about their safety: The farmers had guns and they were drunk. "What should we do?" she asked Lars, not sure how to handle the situation. There was no way to tell how these armed, drunken farmers would act toward the group.

"Wait and see," Lars said, staying cool. Like Beth, Lars is an expert kayaker. He doesn't get scared very easily.

That night the farmers made a big fire. They sat beside it and drank vodka, which is a Russian liquor made from rye or wheat. In Russian, the farmers began talking about a tourist they had killed the year before, and Beth overheard them.

"I got really scared," Beth said. "It was the top of the mountain. It was dark. And it seemed like the more they drank, the angrier they got." She moved back from the fire and motioned for the others to follow. She told them what she had heard.

"Do you think they'll kill us?" Renee asked. She looked frightened.

"I don't know," Beth replied.

Just then, the farmers noticed that Beth and her friends had disappeared.

One of them charged over. He was very mad. "Where are you hiding your vodka?" he screamed. Beth and Vanya confronted them. Beth calmly told the farmer that her group didn't have any. Her new attitude about turning fear into a positive thing was having quite an effect on her. She and Vanya kept up their brave front. "If you want vodka," they suggested, "you should get back in your tractor and drive back down the mountain to buy some."

To the paddlers' great surprise, that's exactly what the farmers did.

3 * Feeling Sheepish

Beth and her friends woke up the next morning, glad to be alive. But their joy didn't last long. The temperature dropped so much that it didn't feel like summer to Beth. One look at the dark clouds overhead told them it was going to snow. They put on their packs quickly and began hiking toward the river. The trail went on for miles. It took them down toward a valley, then to the top of another mountain. For two more days they followed it, hiking deeper and deeper into the Altai Mountains. The weather got colder and colder. The snow looked like it would come at any time.

For Beth, it was frustrating to be in Russia, but still not on the river. Yet something unexpected was taking place. The trip wasn't her dream journey, but it was making her very happy. "There's an old saying," she philosophized, "that the destination isn't as important as the journey. I found that the journey I was taking toward the river was much more interesting than if we'd just flown in and begun kayaking right away."

The next part of their adventure happened when the group was hiking up yet another mountain trail and came across a lonely old shepherd tending a large, spread-out flock.

"Hello," Beth shouted to him, surprised to see someone living alone so far from a village.

The shepherd stared at the group. He must have wondered what in the world a group of Americans was doing up there.

"What's the fastest way to the Sumulta River?" Beth asked him. She listened as the shepherd described in great detail how they could get to the pass that would lead them over the mountain and into the valley in which the Sumulta was nestled. "At the top of the pass, there is a shepherd's cabin," he told them as they thanked him and began to go on their way. "Feel free to sleep in there tonight."

They didn't make it to the cabin before dark, so they pitched their tents under the stars. They had climbed so high up the mountain that they were above the treeline. That meant there wasn't enough oxygen at that altitude for trees to live, so the ground was bare and rocky. It wasn't the best place to camp, but as Beth went to sleep, she dreamed once more of guiding her kayak down the wild Sumulta.

When she woke up, Beth was colder than she had ever been in her life. It was as though someone had put her sleeping bag in a freezer! Outside the tent, she could hear the wind blowing hard and fast. She unzipped the tent to look outside, but couldn't see anything but snow.

"Blizzard!" she yelled, waking up the others.

Quickly, Beth and her friends packed their gear and raced toward the mountain top. "Most of the clothes that we brought with us were for summer," Beth said later. "We didn't have clothes for snow." Their only hope for survival was to make it to the shepherd's cabin. "We did not know where it was, but we knew we had to find it."

With snow and wind ripping through their thin summer clothes, the group marched quickly. They kept going, but didn't see the cabin. The snow began falling so hard that Beth was afraid they might not be able to see the cabin and walk right past it. Just when it seemed they could go no further, the cabin came into sight. It wasn't much — just a shelter, really — but seeing it filled them with joy. They bundled inside happily and waited for the storm to pass.

Two days later, the blizzard stopped, but the four feet of snow outside made going on impossible. The thick clouds overhead meant that a rescue helicopter, even if they were able to get in touch with one, wouldn't be able to see them. So until the snow melted, they were stuck.

Oleg stood up as the group huddled inside the small cabin. He was wearing a thin pair of warmups and thin rubber sandals. "I will run back to Gorno-Altaysk," he said bravely. "And telephone for a rescue helicopter to pick us up." The others tried to talk him out of it. They reminded him of how cold it was outside and how thin his clothes were. He wasn't even wearing socks! But Oleg had made up his mind. He argued that he could run

Helicopters are often used for rescues on mountains because they can land in places where regular planes can't. And if even the helicopter can't land, it can hover above people, and a rope can be dropped down so the people can climb up.

down the mountain much quicker than the whole group could walk with all their equipment. Then he stepped outside the door and began picking his way down the mountain as best he could. The others could do nothing in the meantime but wait.

To pass the time, Beth read a novel. She tried not to worry. "You have to remember, we were not only stranded, but we were running out of food," she pointed out later. "We had no way of getting off the mountain top."

On the third day, Beth heard the distant sound of footsteps crunching through the snow. She poked her head out the door. There, trailing his flock behind him, was the shepherd!

"I have a gift for you," he explained when he drew closer.

Beth, who was hungry enough to eat a Clydesdale horse, hoped the gift meant food. In fact, the shepherd offered them one of his flock.

No one in the group knew what to say. The sheep would make a fine meal, and they were thankful for it. But they had nothing to give him in return.

"Beth," Renee said with a nudge, "give him your book."

"My book?! I'm only halfway done," Beth protested.

Beth looked at the shepherd. She held the book in one hand. It was written in English and there was no way he would ever understand a word of it. But Beth knew what it was like to receive a gift from a faraway place. The poor old shepherd probably would never have another chance to get a souvenir from America.

Slowly, she extended the book. "Here," she said.

After the shepherd took the book and gleefully began making his way down the mountain, Beth and the others eyed the sheep. What, they wondered, was the best way to kill it and cook it?

Caroline stepped forward. Tall and blonde, with square shoulders and a defiant attitude, the San Francisco firefighter pulled the sheep away from the others. "We're not eating him," she said firmly.

"Caroline," Beth pointed out delicately. "We're starving here. If we don't eat that sheep, we could die."

"Haven't you ever heard of animal rights?" replied Caroline.

"You would rather starve to death than eat this sheep?" Beth asked.

"I don't think that's so strange," Caroline retorted.

The group looked at Caroline, trying to decide what to do. Beth knew that when Caroline made up her mind to do something, she could be very stubborn. Once, the two of them had run a river together in Australia. Caroline's fierce determination helped them through a section of white water known as "Deadman's Drop" that nobody had ever gone down before.

Looking at Caroline arguing for the sheep's life, Beth saw the same resolve and fire as when they made the "Drop." Beth knew then that she wouldn't be having lamb chops for dinner.

The next morning, the skies cleared. Soon the sounds

of a rescue helicopter filled the air. Oleg had done it! Setting down on the mountain top, the crew loaded Beth and the others aboard. The plan was to fly the group directly to the Sumulta River. As the helicopter lifted slowly into the air, Caroline settled into her seat. There was no fire in her eyes, only happiness.

Resting contentedly on the floor of the helicopter was the sheep.

4 * PUTTING IN

The river, at last! Beth stood on a rocky beach next to the Sumulta and was filled with wonder. She watched the clear water flowing past and couldn't wait to begin paddling on it. After the cold, bare mountains, she loved seeing the thick green forest along the riverbank and feeling the sun so warm and pleasant on her face.

Beth thought of her friend Jaroslav as she watched the river roll on. Downstream there would be rapids and waterfalls that might hold her underwater and try to take her life, too. She tried to remain calm. "This was going to be the first time I was out on the river since Jaroslav died. And even though our group would be the first people to run the upper reaches of the Sumulta — which is scary because you never know what's around the next corner — I wasn't nervous or scared. It's just that when I thought of Jaroslav, it gave me pause. If it happened to him, it could happen to anybody."

The group put their boats in the water the next

morning. Six Russians from Project RAFT joined Beth and her group (the lamb was given to a shepherd who lived by the Sumulta), at the river. Another group of six Americans also met them there. The Russians brought rafts instead of kayaks. Although bigger and slower than kayaks, the advantage of rafts is that more people can be in the boat at the same time.

With all the new people, Beth's quiet little white water expedition had turned into a great, big, international party.

"The great thing about the Russians is not only that they're so tough, but that all of them like to sing and play the guitar," Beth marveled. "Every night during the trip when we got off the river, we would sit around the campfire and play the guitar and sing songs. It was like summer camp or something."

Things weren't so lighthearted during the day. Running rapids is serious stuff.

The only sound on the river is the roar of white water as it squeezes through rocks and boulders. When paddlers communicate on the river, they have to yell as loud as they can to be heard. When paddlers speak different languages, river commands may be the only words they have in common. "I think the only words in English that some of those Russians understood were 'forward paddle, back paddle, right turn, and left turn,'" Beth says.

The kayaks led the way. Paddling next to Lars, Beth felt tension, fear, and anxiety building inside her. She tried to push these feelings aside, but they kept coming back. "There's a really strange feeling you get in the pit of your stomach when you're the first person to run a river," Beth says. "Anything can happen at any time. You could all of a sudden be pinned by some rocks, for instance." This is one of the worst hazards that a kayaker faces. It occurs when a pile of boulders lies at the bottom of a waterfall. Water, of course, just bounces off the boulders and continues on downstream. But if a kayaker gets caught, his or her boat will be crushed immediately — and the kayaker with it.

"The first two days on the water were easy," remembers Beth. "I just played in the white water." But on the third day, the river began to move faster as it narrowed to squeeze through a tall canyon. "When a river gets squeezed like that, it creates my favorite kind of rapids: tight and steep. The white water gets big. I just love it because there's no room in that kind of situation for your mind to wander."

The rapids in the canyon were a mile long. Because rafts are clumsier than kayaks, it was agreed that the rafters would stay behind. If the kayakers could navigate the rapids safely, then the rafters would follow. Beth and Lars began to paddle cautiously into the rapids.

"You ready?" Beth yelled to him.

"Yeah," he shouted back, nodding his head.

"Then let's do it," she replied.

Beth dug her paddle hard into the river. Almost immediately, her boat plunged off of a big drop and she was in the middle of frothing white water. Cold spray coated her face. Her hair felt wet beneath her helmet.

One of the key elements in maintaining control in white water is speed in going over the drops, so Beth began paddling as fast as she could. She skirted left, away from a boulder as big as a house. She paddled again, harder this time. Beth didn't know where Lars was, but it didn't matter. Another plunge, this one bigger. Beth didn't see it coming and didn't have time to lean back in the boat to keep her balance. At the bottom of the plunge, she almost tipped over. Somehow, she managed to keep her balance and paddle on.

The roar of the white water grew louder with every paddle stroke deeper into the canyon. It felt like it echoed inside of Beth's head. She back-paddled to maneuver around a small tree that popped up out of nowhere. Trees sometimes scared her more than boulders. At least boulders were smooth. If you fell out of the boat, you would just bounce hard off the boulder and get swept downstream. With trees, your life jacket could get stuck on an underwater branch and you might not be able to get loose. The only thing to think about as the water pushed you under and pounded hard on your chest, was whether or not the rescuers would be able to find your body.

Beth didn't have time for thoughts like that. She took a moment to get out of her kayak and scout the river from the shore. After climbing back in and getting out on the river, she heard the telltale roar of an upcoming waterfall. Beth paddled hard toward the edge of the falls.

She wasn't scared. She knew just what to do.

As the kayak was about to launch over the edge, Beth leaned way back, so far that the back of her head was almost touching the hard plastic shell of the kayak. Like a torpedo, the kayak flew off the waterfall. She took a deep breath and held it. Beth felt herself falling, falling, falling. The cold slap of icy river water drenched her as the kayak plunged in, going all the way under the surface. The waterfall's force held Beth under. It was loud down there, loud and cold. Beth tried not to be scared. She just concentrated on staying calm.

As the kayak bobbed to the surface, Beth immediately began looking for the next obstacle.

"Remember, Beth," she told herself, "nobody has ever run this river before. You don't know what might happen."

But the worst of the rapids was behind her. Soon the canyon widened and the water became calm and gentle. Beth paddled over to the shore and waited for Lars. Leaving their boats, the two of them walked upstream to where the rafters waited.

"How was it?" Caroline asked quickly. She and Renee were going to raft with the Russians.

"It was . . . awesome," Beth replied, giving Caroline a high-five. "It was really awesome."

"Do you want to do it again?" Caroline asked.

"What do you mean?" Beth replied. After what she had just been through, she'd have to be crazy to try it again. Looking in Caroline's eyes, she could see the determined look making its way in.

"I mean, since you know the way down, why don't you guide us in one of the rafts?"

Beth thought about it. She hadn't been in a raft in three years. It might be crazy, but still, that rapids had been a whole lot of fun. Beth looked at Caroline and smiled. "Yeah, sure."

So Beth Rypins did it all one more time.

5 * Back to Barnaul

After four days on the water, Beth was loving the trip more than ever. The white water was great, the campfires were fun, and she was over her anxiety about the river. She felt strong and powerful.

The morning of the fifth day, Beth was eating breakfast next to the fire. Everybody else was there, too. Lyosha, one of the Russians, stood up slowly. He had a serious look on his face. "My friends," he began carefully. "My friends, on this day, three years ago, my brother died on the river."

As he talked, Beth thought of Jaroslav and became very sad. "My brother was a great man," Lyosha continued. "And it is a Russian tradition that we celebrate his life each year on the day he died. As a special meal, today we will eat rice and raisins and drink vodka in his memory."

Beth thought again of Jaroslav. Then she began to wonder why it was that she found it so important to be a kayaker. She knew she loved doing it, but why did she love doing it so much? "I think that when you get to the top of any extreme sport, you begin to like walking the edge," she realized. "On one side of the edge is life. On the other side is death. I think we all know someone who has gone over the edge."

That day on the river, everybody was sad. Tensions were running high as the group followed the river into another canyon. "This one was even tighter than before," Beth remembers. Big round boulders filled the narrow river. When white water bounced off the boulders, it created huge waves.

Beth went down the rapids first. "The current was so strong that I knew I had to be very aggressive if I was going to make it," she said later. Halfway through, Beth spotted a giant boulder in the middle of the river. It was the biggest boulder she had ever seen in her life. It was so huge that it split the river in half. "If you went to the right side of the boulder, you were safe," Beth says. "It was a clear drop. But if you went to the left, the river was choked up with lots of rocks."

Beth went right. After she kayaked all the way down the canyon, Beth walked back up to tell Caroline about the boulder. "Make sure you paddle hard going into that boulder. And no matter what you do, stay to the right. That's very important. Make sure you stay to the right."

Caroline nodded her head. She would be rafting with a Russian named Zhenya *{ZEN-ya}*.

Beth walked back downstream toward her kayak. On

the way, she stopped on shore near the big boulder and waited for Caroline and Zhenya. She could see them in the distance as they approached. Quickly and carefully, they rowed toward the boulder. Suddenly, Beth got worried. Zhenya had earned a reputation on the trip for being smart but wild. She knew he liked doing things the hard way.

"I could see that they were going toward the left side," she says. "I was furious." She started yelling at them, but they couldn't hear her. As Zhenya and Caroline paddled harder and harder toward the rocks, Beth could only stand there and watch. All the emotions of earlier in the day came up again. "I felt so out of control. There was absolutely nothing I could do."

Caroline and Zhenya disappeared behind the boulder. Beth hoped that they weren't being pounded on the rocks, but she knew they probably were. Overwhelmed with sadness, she could only stare at the river.

Then she saw them. Not only were they alive, but they were paddling their raft downstream, fighting their way through some more rapids. "I found out later that Zhenya had an instinct about the left side. He thought maybe it wasn't so bad after all."

Later that night, Caroline and Beth talked about the incident. "I could see you were worried, but there was nothing I could do," Caroline said.

"Why didn't you argue with him?" Beth asked angrily.

Caroline was quiet for a second before answering. "As

good as you are, Beth, I'm surprised you don't know that it's useless to argue on a river."

"What do you mean?" Beth asked. "Of course you can argue. Zhenya was trying to make the river as hard as possible. That could have killed you."

"Beth, listen to me: It doesn't do any good to argue on a river because the river always wins," Caroline replied.

Beth thought about that. She smiled and gave her friend a big hug. "I'm just glad you're OK."

That would be their last day on the Sumulta River. The next morning, they reached the point where the Sumulta flows into the Katun River, of which it is a tributary. The Katun is a wide, slow river. With sadness, Beth realized the trip was coming to an end. Soon, they would all be literally halfway around the world from each other. The Americans would get back to Barnaul, fly to Moscow, then fly home to San Francisco.

From her kayak, Beth gazed across the river at the fleet of kayaks and rafts. When she left her home three weeks before, all she wanted to do was find some quiet time. With a smile, she reflected that she hadn't had a single quiet moment on the entire trip. She had almost been thrown in jail, shot, trapped in a blizzard, starved to death, and thrown into a raging rapids.

So what began as a relaxing getaway had turned into an adventure. "Isn't that the way it always is?" Beth reminded herself. With that, she dug her paddle in the water and began her journey home.

SAILING BLIND

ONE MAN'S COURAGEOUS CROSSING OF THE PACIFIC OCEAN

1 * Hurricane

Hank Dekker was waking up very slowly. What he really wanted to do was go back to sleep, but he had the feeling that something wasn't quite right. "What could possibly be the matter?" he thought groggily. He could taste blood in his mouth and feel that his thick cotton socks were cold and wet. "Maybe some water splashed inside the cabin," he reasoned. After all, he was in his sailboat, in the middle of the Pacific Ocean, a little less than halfway between San Francisco and Hawaii. It was only natural that a little salt water might wash in. He rolled over and tried to go back to sleep.

But the feeling wouldn't go away. So far it had been an easy voyage. Hank, who had been legally blind for six years, had set an ambititous goal: to be the first blind sailor to venture across the ocean alone. And though the Pacific Ocean seemed endlessly vast, so far it had been gentle. He was even letting the self-steering equipment guide the boat tonight, which was something he didn't do unless he was sure of perfect weather. If there was even the slightest chance of bad seas, he would stay awake and steer the boat himself.

"That's strange," he thought next, trying to get comfortable in his bunk. "Wasn't I sleeping on top of the cushion?"

Sure enough, the cushion on which he had fallen asleep three hours before was now on top of him. In fact, he was sleeping against the side of the boat, called the hull. If he had been in his bedroom at home, it would have been like waking up on the side of a wall. "A porthole [window] must have broken," he thought groggily. He was still half-asleep. Just then, a tremendous thump rolled his boat — a 24-footer named *Dark Star* — hard to one side. Gallons of water gushed in the broken porthole and soaked him to the skin.

That's when the realization hit him like a two-fisted punch in the gut: "I'm sinking!"

It was true. Just nine days into his 2,400-mile passage, Hank had sailed smack into Hurricane Henrietta. *Dark Star* was lying on her side, filling quickly with water. "I knew Henrietta was approaching, but I thought

Hank Dekker likes the feeling of control he gets when he's sailing.

BILL EPPRIDGE

it was too far away to reach me. I was wrong," he remembers grimly. "The worst thing was the wind. I could hear it out there making this horrible screaming and screeching.

"What had happened to *Dark Star* was that she had surfed down a wave," Hank explains. "When she got to the bottom, she broached [turned sideways to the waves]. Then a wave went right over the top of her and knocked her down." That was the thump Hank had heard.

The waves around him had been whipped up to about 25 feet high. In hurricanes and other big storms, they can get even higher! The best thing to do when caught in

such rough seas is to take most, if not all, of the sails down and steer the boat in the same direction as the waves are traveling. That way, the boat surfs down the front of the wave. The danger comes when a sailboat broaches, because when the boat turns sideways to the waves, it is absorbing the wave's power at the boat's widest point: its side. When that happens, the boat can get knocked down on its side, or turn upside down. The sails can fill with water and the weight will work like an anchor to keep the boat from righting herself. If the sails have been taken down, the boat is often able to turn rightside up by herself.

As Hank woke up and took stock of the situation, he

remembered that he had left one of *Dark Star's* two sails up when he went to sleep. It was the jib, the smaller of the two and the one located at the front of the boat. (The larger sail is called a mainsail.)

"The jib was under water," Hank recalled. "I realized that if I didn't get outside the boat and release the jib, *Dark Star* would sink." To do that, Hank would have to make his way out of the cabin. He would be exposed to the wind and waves as he untied the jib sheet, which is the rope that attaches the bottom of the jib to the boat. It would be a very hard thing for any person to do. Because of his blindness, it would be even tougher for Hank.

Struggling to his feet, Hank opened the hatch, a small doorway leading from the cabin to the deck. Water poured in immediately. He fought his way through it. Slowly and carefully, he inched outside. He used his hands to search for the jib sheet. Hank found it and quickly untied it. The jib was free! "*Dark Star* slowly began swinging upright. Slowly, slowly, slowly — then she went straight up," Hank says with an air of relief. "Man, it's a good feeling when your boat's standing straight up in the water."

But Hank wasn't out of trouble yet. There were two feet of water inside the boat. Worse, the jib was flapping wildly in the wind. Although it wasn't attached to the deck anymore, it was attached to the headstay, a wire rope than runs from the bow of the boat to the top of the mast. The headstay helps hold up the mast, which is the part of a boat that sticks straight up from the deck like a flagpole. Hank knew right away that if the jib kept flapping like that, it would put enough tension on the headstay to pull down *Dark Star's* mast. If that happened, *Dark Star* wouldn't be able to sail anymore. She would just bob in the water like a cork in a giant bathtub.

Hank decided that the jib was more urgent than the water in the cabin. He carefully crawled up onto the deck again. In a situation like this, sailors usually wear a safety line that attaches them to the boat. Hank, however, couldn't find his. If one strong wave hit, he could be washed overboard and his life would be over. "It felt like it took me an hour to get out there to the jib," he recalled. "For every one foot I moved forward, a wave washed me one foot back."

He made it, though. With practiced finesse, Hank pulled the jib down. Then he scurried back to get all the water out of his cabin. Furiously, he dumped bucket after bucket from the boat. When he was finished, there was nothing to do but stay below in the cabin and wait for the storm to pass.

For the next two days he listened to *Dark Star* get pounded by wave after wave. She rolled over again several times. However, without the jib to drag it down, she popped right back up.

On the third day, the sun came out. Hank went on deck again. "All storms pass," Hank states, "and that one did too." He quickly checked his special navigational gear. If any of it was broken, he was in big trouble. Hank depends on special equipment that actually talks, telling him which direction he's headed in. Without that equipment, Hank would be stuck. He was more than 1,400 miles from Hawaii.

Navigation is the science of determining what a boat's or plane's position is, and what course or direction should be taken to get to a chosen place.

As Hank explored the gear, his worst fears were realized. His talking equipment was broken and filled with water. He had no way of knowing which way Hawaii was. He had a ship-to-shore radio, but he was too far away from land to use it. With a sigh, Hank sat down and began trying to think of a solution.

2 * INTO THE DARKNESS

Hank hasn't always been blind. In the first 37 years of his life, he could see. At one point, he even drove race cars as a hobby. "I loved racing," he remembers. "I think that's why I enjoy sailing so much. I love being in control of the boat just like I used to love being in control of the race car." Hank had 20-10 eyesight then, which is very good. Twenty-ten means that he could see things from 20 feet away that people with normal eyes couldn't see until they were 10 feet away.

Hank lived in Honolulu, Hawaii then. He was a very successful businessman, working as the general manager of a car dealership. He and his wife had two children: a daughter named Kim and a son named Mike.

Hank was a coach of Mike's Little League baseball team. "I was living the American Dream," Hank says fondly. "I had everything in life that I could ever want. I was extremely happy."

One day in 1972, Hank was playing catch with Mike's team. Hank noticed that he was having trouble seeing the ball. He couldn't see anything thrown to his left or his right. In fact, sometimes he couldn't even see balls that were thrown too high or too low. Hank could only see the ball when it was thrown directly at him. His view of the world was mysteriously narrowing.

Right away, Hank went to see an opthamologist (an eye doctor) to have his sight checked. What the doctor discovered was terrible: Hank had glaucoma *{glaw-KOH-muh}*. "I was crushed when I found out," Hank says with understatement. "Totally crushed."

Glaucoma is a disease affecting the eye caused by increased pressure within the eye itself. This continued high pressure damages the sensitive optic nerve fibers unless victims are treated early on. Untreated glaucoma victims eventually go blind. Regular eye exams can pick up the presence of the disease.

Hoping to correct the problem with surgery, Hank moved his family from Hawaii to Connecticut. The best eye hospitals in the world are in Connecticut and the nearby New York area. But after many operations and special treatments, Hank's sight was still getting worse. "My field of vision was getting so narrow that if I read the word 'the' on a piece of paper, I could see the letter 't' and had to turn my head to see the letter 'h'." Then Hank received a phone call from his doctor. He wanted Hank and his wife to come see him at his office. Hank was frightened when he got the call because he knew what the doctor might say to them.

"Have a seat, please," the doctor said when Hank and his wife arrived. He liked Hank, and didn't feel very good about what he was about to tell him.

Hank and his wife sat down. The doctor sat across a desk from them. More than anything else, Hank hoped the doctor would tell him that he had found a miraculous way to cure Hank's glaucoma.

The doctor got right to the point. "You're going blind, Hank. There's nothing more that I, nor anyone else, can do for you. You'll just have to get used to it and start planning for it."

Hank stumbled out of the doctor's office. He thought of all the things he liked to do that he wouldn't be able to do anymore: Take his kids fishing, drive race cars, coach Little League, and many other things. He thought of sunsets he would never see. He would never watch a movie again or even walk around a strange room without bumping into furniture. A hatred filled Hank as he walked out of the office that day. He despised everyone in the world who had the ability to see. He even felt hatred for his children. "I fell apart at that moment," Hank realizes when he looks back. "I became very bitter. It was the first time in my life I'd faced adversity and I couldn't handle it."

One way Hank showed that he couldn't handle the situation was that he started drinking liquor too much. He quit his job. He began yelling at his wife and children all time, taking his anger out on them. Slowly, Hank began losing touch with reality and sinking into a swamp of self-pity and depression. Hank went from being a successful businessman to being an angry, violent drunk. His own children were so afraid of Hank that they couldn't stand being in the same house with him anymore.

On a morning that Hank will never forget, the family decided it was time to confront him about his behavior. When he came down to breakfast, his daughter, Kim, who was 9, looked at him with tears in her eyes. She didn't see her father at the table: She saw a very mean person. "Daddy," she said to him, using words that she had practiced saying. "We care that you're going blind, but you're not nice to be with. I don't want you to be my Daddy anymore."

Hank's wife and son agreed: They wanted him out of the house forever. Hank promised to change. He begged their forgiveness and said he would work at being his old self again. For a week he tried to accept his blindness and not be so angry about it. He pretended to be happy whenever his family was around. But soon he was angry and violent once more. Sadly, the day came when Hank was forced to leave. He loaded all his possessions into his car. Despite the fact that his vision was now extremely limited, he drove off, trying to get as far away as he possibly could. He headed west, and when he finally ended up in San Francisco, California, Hank stopped. Before him lay the Pacific Ocean.

He could go no further — or so he thought.

3 * HOMELESS TO HOPEFUL

Hank tried to get his act together when he got to San Francisco. It was easy at first: "I got a job right away at a [car] dealership, working as general manager. But I soon found out that I couldn't keep a job because I was still drinking and not accepting my blindness. I was fired from that job. The next job I got wasn't as good. Soon I got fired from that job. And on it went, me getting hired and fired, until I got down to the very last job. I was working in a used car lot, washing cars. They'd throw me a couple bucks for every car I'd wash. Behind my back they'd tell jokes and laugh at me [because I couldn't see]. Finally, I just said the heck with it and I quit working altogether."

Without a job, Hank couldn't afford to pay his rent anymore. Soon he was homeless and living on the streets of San Francisco. At night he slept in an abandoned sewer pipe. During the day, he got drunk whenever he could and took naps on the sidewalk. He stopped caring about how he looked and never changed his clothes. He didn't cut his hair or shave.

"If you think in your mind of the most miserable-looking homeless person you could ever imagine, then that was me," Hank says. "I was totally filthy, I smelled awful, and I drank all the time. When I got hungry, I used to go into dumpsters to find trash I could eat."

After a year of being homeless and blind, Hank wanted a change. "I realized that I was trying to kill myself. What's more, I was trying to do it in the most degrading way I knew how." He was tired of drinking and sleeping on the street. The successful man inside him wanted to be respected again.

One day, Hank was taken to the hospital after getting

into a fight with another homeless person. A doctor there was just about to start a therapy program designed to help blind people deal with their handicap. "I only agreed to go because it was winter, you know?" Hank says. "It was cold outside and this was a good way to come inside and get a free cup of coffee."

Although it seems hard to believe, the other people in the group were the first blind people he had ever spoken with. Just talking with them made Hank feel better about himself. "Basically," Hank says, "it was truth therapy. We were all professional people who had lost all hope when we lost our sight. Most of us had lost our spouses and our families and our jobs. We all drank a little too much. And we were all afraid to use the cane because we were afraid of looking vulnerable." After that first meeting, Hank looked forward to meeting with the group.

Some blind people use a special cane when they walk. They sweep it back and forth in front of them to keep them from bumping into things.

The effect of the group was overwhelming. Hank began taking care of himself. He took his disability benefits (money paid by the government to help people with disabilities) and instead of buying liquor, he used the money to rent a small room. He started shaving and showering. Instead of eating garbage, he bought nutritious food because he could now afford it. A month later he was ready to go looking for a job again. Instead of being filthy, he was clean and well-groomed. He could even joke a little bit about being blind.

Hank soon landed a job working for an organization known as Lighthouse for the Blind. Lighthouse specializes in selling products like plant boxes and brooms that are made by blind people. Hank's job was called marketing. That meant he was in charge of finding companies willing to buy the things Lighthouse employees made. Because he had been a salesman before, Hank was perfect for the job. He became a success again. "After I had been working there awhile, we had such a demand for blind products that we couldn't keep up with it," Hanks says.

Within a year, life was much better for Hank. He went from being homeless to being in charge of 35 employees. He moved from his cheap room into a big Victorian house in a good part of San Francisco. He started a small company called California Association of Services by the Handicapped, which sold products made by blind people and provided a janitorial service. Most important, he once again got in contact with his two children back in Connecticut.

In the fall of 1980, life got even better for Hank. That was when he first went sailing. "A friend of mine rented a boat one weekend. It was a small boat — 19-foot, I think. We took it for a sail in San Francisco Bay. I just fell in love with sailing immediately. I got to steer the boat for awhile and it was great. When I first put my hand on the tiller (a lever used to steer a boat), it reminded me of driving a car. There's a feeling of control that I really hadn't experienced since I became blind."

Hank and his friend, who was not blind, went sailing again the next week, this time on a 24-foot boat. Hank began to imagine what it would be like to have a boat of his very own. "I thought, 'If I buy a boat, I can set it up just the way I want it so I know where everything is. Then I can be the skipper and give orders to people who come sailing with me.'"

Before he bought a boat, Hank wanted to learn as much about boats and sailing as he could. He raced to the library and checked out all the audiotapes he could find about sailing (many books are converted into audiotapes by the Library of Congress in Washington and other organizations). And Hank was interested not only in tapes about how to sail, but also in the theories behind sailing: things like how a sail worked and how to navigate. He got tapes about famous sailors and their voyages across the oceans of the world.

By the time Hank finally bought a boat, he knew a lot about sailing and had spent a lot of time out on the water sailing with his friend.

The boat he chose was a 24-footer with a small cabin fitted to sleep two and a small galley (kitchen). Hank gave her the name *Dark Star*. He rented a slip (a parking space for a boat) for her in a San Francisco marina and was soon spending every spare moment sailing. "Within six months," he recalls, "I was a better sailor than any of my friends."

It was hard to believe, but it was true. He had practiced a lot. Because Hank couldn't see, he had learned to sail by using a Braille compass and relying on his other senses. He can feel whether a sail is full of air by how much pressure there is on the line. Using his sense of touch, Hank steers the tiller smoothly and efficiently. He can sense an incoming storm before clouds came over the horizon by noting a drop in temperature or how much moisture is in the air. "I felt like sailing was making me a whole man again," he reflects.

> Braille is a system of writing and printing for the blind. Patterns of raised dots represent letters and numbers. The raised dots can be identified by light touches of the fingertips.

Hank and a friend were on board *Dark Star* one afternoon, lazing in the sun as she glided through San Francisco Bay. Hank was in love with the sea that day. In his mind, he tried to picture how wonderful it must have been for the great explorers to sail across the ocean.

"You know," Hank said dreamily, "I think it would be great to sail across the ocean alone. To get out there and set your sails and not hit land for thousands of miles."

His friend laughed. "You could never do that. You've only been sailing for a year. People who sail across the ocean have to have years of sailing experience." What Hank's friend was also thinking was that blind people can't sail across the ocean alone. It had never been done before. There was no reason to think a sailor of Hank's limited ability could do it.

"The heck with you," Hank said angrily. "Maybe you can't do it, but I can. Someday I'm going to sail this boat from here to Honolulu."

Just saying the words made Hank happy. In his mind, he imagined how wonderful it would be to sail *Dark Star* into Honolulu Harbor. Because he had lived there before, he could imagine the clear blue color of the water there, and the warmth of tropical breezes on his face. He could see the immense green silhouette of Diamond Head volcano marking the entrance to the harbor.

"Yes, indeed," Hank repeated. "I'm going to do it."

His friend laughed again. "You'll never make it."

Hank said his goal aloud a final time. "I will sail this boat from here to Honolulu, and I will do it within the next two years," he stated firmly. But despite his confidence, Hank wondered if it was really possible. Many experts said he couldn't do it. He wondered to himself whether it was really smart for a blind person to try sailing the ocean alone.

He decided it was. "When I made up my mind to sail across the Pacific Ocean, I realized it was the first time in my life I had ever set a goal for myself," Hank says. "I was determined to see that goal come true."

4 * Chasing the Goal

Hank was a pretty good sailor when he decided to sail across the Pacific. However, he knew he wouldn't be able to do it unless he was more than good — he needed to be great. And the only way to become a great sailor was to practice. That meant sailing had to become his life. There was just one problem: He didn't have time. Working all day during the week left only the evenings and weekends for sailing. So Hank solved the problem: He quit his job. Soon he was sailing each and every day, sometimes as many as 18 hours at a time. Unlike most sailors, Hank didn't have to worry about being out on the water too late and coming into port when night fell. For Hank, it was always night.

To make money, Hank bought something called a charter service. For a fee, he gave people sailboat rides. "I'd get six or seven people on board," he says with a laugh, "and I'd wait until we were fifty yards away from the dock before telling them I was blind. Usually they'd look at me kind of funny and go 'You're jokin', right?' When I told them I wasn't, they got scared until they realized I knew how to sail pretty good. Even then, they were usually pretty scared." Eventually, the Coast Guard informed Hank he needed a license for his charter business and Hank knew right away he couldn't pass the eye exam for the license. He ultimately had to shut down the business.

Along with daily practice, Hank prepared for his voyage by getting together the equipment he would need for a long voyage. He needed everything from special navigational aids to tell him where he was, to water containers, to new sails. To chart his course, he had a girlfriend use something that looks like a pizza cutter, a wheel with a bumpy edge mounted on a handle. She flipped over the nautical maps, which are called charts, and used the wheel to press the bumps into places on the chart to mark things like latitude and longitude lines and the outlines of the coast. These bumps allowed Hank to "read" the chart.

In addition to the Braille compass, Hank had a special Loran (which stands for Long Range Navigation) device. "Hello, captain," the Loran would say when Hank typed a message into it. "Where are we going?" The Loran had a flat, electronic voice. Hank would feed it information through a keyboard, and the Loran's voice would tell him the exact latitude and longitude of *Dark Star*. With that information, he could consult his charts to plot, or figure out, the best route to Hawaii. Navigation, it appeared, would be the least of Hank's worries.

The Loran navigation system, which is no longer widely used, is a system of radio navigation that helps boats and planes find their positions. The boat or plane has a receiver that gets signals from stations on land. It measures the amount of time between signals to figure out the position of the boat on a chart.

The problem of high seas was another matter entirely. Hank knew that waves in San Francisco Bay weren't big enough to prepare him for sailing the Pacific. So he decided to do a practice voyage. His plan was to sail *Dark Star* along the Pacific coast north to Canada. Then sail south down the coast to

Mexico. In Mexico, he would turn around and come home. The entire practice journey would be almost 2,500 miles long.

Hank set out on his practice voyage in the winter of 1982. Staying at least 30 miles offshore, he made his way up to Canada and back down to Mexico just fine. The weather was calm and the sea was relatively peaceful. He turned around and headed back. Though Hank was gaining valuable single-handed ocean experience, he was not seeing big waves or bad weather.

But that soon changed. A severe storm struck when he was less than 150 miles from reaching home in San Francisco. Pounding waves and 80 mile-per-hour winds rocked *Dark Star*. Hank stayed below in the cabin. He kept all the hatches and portholes closed tightly so water couldn't get in. Sure of himself and his boat, Hank kept the sails down and rode out the storm. When it passed, he calmly navigated those last miles into the slip in San Francisco. The trip up from Mexico should have taken just two days but ended up lasting eight. Still, when it was all done, Hank was convinced he was ready to sail the Pacific alone.

Hank decided that his trip to Honolulu would take place the next summer. "I spent the winter working on *Dark Star*," Hank recalls. "Every spare amount of money and time I had went into preparing her for the voyage." He plugged leaks and gave her a fresh new coat of blue paint. He checked all the sails for rips and tears. He arranged the cabin to fit the six weeks worth of food and water he planned to carry. Hank checked and re-checked his charts, compass, and Loran to make sure there were no flaws.

Finally the day came to set sail for Honolulu. It was July 27, 1983. Hank let some friends tow him out of San Francisco Bay behind a power boat. Everybody laughed and made nervous jokes about the trip ahead. They took pictures and said things like "I wish I was brave enough to do what you're doing." Hank was filled with pride. Less than three years before, Hank had been homeless and drunk. He had no pride then, and nothing to live for. Now he was sailing alone across the ocean.

"Ready, Hank?" His friends on the power boat called out. They were outside San Francisco Bay and ready to untie the rope that connected them.

"Ready," he called back. And he was.

The tow rope was reeled in. The power boat turned and chugged back into the Bay. The people on deck looked back at *Dark Star*. She was bobbing in the water with no sails up. The boat wasn't sailing toward Hawaii. In fact, she wasn't sailing anywhere. She was just sitting there. Had Hank changed his mind? Had he chickened out at the last minute?

No. "I sat there on *Dark Star*," Hank remembers. "I could hear the other boat as it left me, and suddenly I was all alone. And at the moment I knew something special. I knew that even if I didn't make it to Hawaii, I had succeeded. Because my goal was to get good enough to make the voyage, and I knew that I was good enough. Just knowing that made me feel really good."

Feeling very content, Hank smiled to himself. He had done it. Keeping that smile on his face, Hank raised the mainsail and pointed *Dark Star* toward Hawaii.

5 * THE CHANNEL BUOY

The day before Hurricane Henrietta struck, Hank was listening to his portable radio. It was just a cheap AM/FM radio, but with it, he could pick up stations more than 1,000 miles away. He found that the music grew stronger when he pointed the radio directly at the city in which the radio station was located. For example, if he pointed it toward Los Angeles, he could hear Los Angeles stations. If he aimed it toward San Francisco, he could hear San Francisco stations — but he couldn't hear the Los Angeles stations anymore.

It was a neat trick, but he didn't think it would ever mean anything.

The day after the hurricane, Hank sat in the cockpit of *Dark Star*. His special equipment had been destroyed. He was calm, but he was worried about how he would navigate to Hawaii. And then he figured it out: He would point the radio toward Hawaii. Even though he was still 1,400 miles away, at least he would know which direction to go. "I could hear this station in Honolulu called K59. I just aimed *Dark Star* toward its sound and set my sails."

A few days later Hank was listening to K59 when he

heard a news report that he was dead. He was upset about it, because he didn't want his friends to think he had died. As the days went past and *Dark Star* drew closer to Hawaii, Hank heard more radio reports about the search for him. He wanted to let people know that he was all right but he was too far away to use his two-way radio. A two-way radio is the kind policemen and firefighters use. It allows people to talk and receive messages. When Hank got close to Hawaii, he would call the Coast Guard and tell them that he was OK. That way people wouldn't worry about him anymore.

In the meantime, Hank once again enjoyed life on the Pacific Ocean. He spent his days steering the boat and fixing anything that was broken. When he wanted to take a bath, he took all his clothes off and scooped water out of the ocean with a big bucket. Then he dumped the bucket over his head. When it was time to sleep, Hank made sure not to sleep for more than 30 minutes to an hour at a time. "Going to sleep for three hours [like he did before the hurricane] is something you just don't do when you sail alone," he says with a shake of his head. He had learned that lesson.

After 22 days at sea, Hank was finally close enough to call the Coast Guard. He called in, identifying himself and his boat.

"Roger, *Dark Star*," came the reply. Then Hank heard a long silence. "Is this the *Dark Star* from California?"

"Yes, it is," Hank said.

"What is your condition, *Dark Star*?" the Coast

Guard wanted to know. They couldn't believe Hank was alive.

Hank told them that he was fine. "Please let the Honolulu Yacht Club know I'll be in tomorrow morning," he said confidently.

There was more silence. "Give us your position, *Dark Star*." The Coast Guard wanted to know where Hank was. But Hank didn't want to tell them. He was afraid that if he told them where he was, they would come out to his boat. If they did that, people might think the Coast Guard showed him the way in. Hank didn't want that. He wanted people to know that he — a blind man — navigated all the way to Hawaii by himself. There was a marker in the water just outside Honolulu Harbor called the Diamond Head Buoy. Hank's goal was to make it to that spot. Once he did that, the Coast Guard could tow him in the rest of the way.

Hank gave the Coast Guard his answer: "I won't tell you."

Hank explained to the Coast Guard why he didn't want to tell them. They understood. Instead of sending a ship to make sure Hank was all right, they agreed to have a plane fly overhead. That way nobody could accuse Hank of following it into Hawaii. A while later, Hank heard an airplane flying over. The roar of its engines was the first sound besides sea and boat noises he had heard in three weeks. "*Dark Star*, *Dark Star*," the pilot radioed to Hank. "We see you. You look pretty good down there."

Hank couldn't believe it. He was really going to do it. Amazingly, his navigation with the little radio had worked! As excited as he was, Hank was still afraid something might go wrong. "That night was the longest night of my life," he recalls. "I was so close to Hawaii. So close to being the first blind man in the history of the world to sail across the ocean alone. I was so afraid that something would go wrong that night and I wouldn't make it. I couldn't sleep a wink. Every time I heard the mast creak, or a line chafe, or a sail flutter, I got worried."

But Hank and *Dark Star* made it through the night just fine. Soon he had definite evidence that he was back in civilization. "The next morning I wanted to make sure I was nice and clean for when we arrived in Honolulu," he recalls. "So I took my clothes off to take a bath and the next thing I know, the ABC News helicopter is flying over."

Hank took his bath anyway. Using the AM/FM radio, Hank started guiding *Dark Star* the final miles to Hawaii. Soon a yacht pulled up next to him. "Hello," they called out. "Congratulations." The yacht tucked in behind *Dark Star*. Other yachts did the same thing.

"I could hear the boats start lining up behind me," he recalls. "They were all considerate and made sure to stay back there so that people didn't think I followed the noise of their engines into the harbor."

When Hank got close enough to Hawaii that he could smell the islands, a final boat pulled up next to him.

"Hank," a voice called out warmly. "I'm from the Honolulu Yacht Club. The Diamond Head Buoy is just 25 yards away. Congratulations, Hank. You made it."

The yachts lined up behind *Dark Star* began blowing their horns. The air was filled with the sound of celebration for Hank and his epic achievement.

"It was a very emotional moment," Hank remembers modestly. "But I didn't want to let go control of the boat yet. I wanted to steer it in." So 10 years after leaving Honolulu to find a cure for his blindness, Hank Dekker was back. "As I guided *Dark Star* toward the Honolulu Yacht Club, I felt as if I could see again. I could see the Diamond Head Buoy very clearly. I could see Diamond Head. I could see the beach-front hotels and the palm trees bowing down before me. I could see clearly the purplish blue of the water change to that lovely aqua as we got closer to shore. But you know, when I finally got to the Yacht Club and stepped out of the boat, I wasn't jumping around like I just won the Olympics. I felt very humbled. It was a very humbling feeling."

Hank has sailed across the Pacific one more time since 1983. His next adventure will be an effort to become the first blind person to sail across the Atlantic Ocean. His boat will leave from New York City and dock at Plymouth, England, a distance of 3,400 miles.

"You know, when I had my sight, I didn't put out," Hank says. "I didn't work hard. Without my sight, I've learned to work to my maximum. I'm actually a better person without my sight."